ROMANCING DR. LINCOLN

AN ALPINE HOSPITAL ROMANCE

ANDREA KATE PEARSON

Romancing Dr. Lincoln

Alpine Hospital Romance

Every Heartbeat Book 3

Andrea Kate Pearson

CHAPTER 1

*C*heryl pushed the off button on her alarm clock, then stared at the dark ceiling of her bedroom, blinking to clear her eyes. Another night of not enough sleep.

Before the busyness of the day overtook her, she allowed herself a few moments to gauge her emotional status. Despite the late bedtime and tossing and turning for the first hour or so, she'd actually slept a little. So that was good. But the melancholy feeling that had overcome her after the movie she and Jade, her fourteen-year-old daughter, had watched the night before still lingered. Love stories always did that to her, specifically ones of younger couples.

Life hadn't turned out the way she'd hoped it would.

With a wave of her hand, Cheryl wiped those thoughts aside and rolled out of bed. She needed to get a move on. Maybe this morning she'd have time for breakfast.

Hope blossomed in her chest, propelling her to go faster through her morning routine, and when she'd left her room, she had just enough time to scramble some eggs and make some toast. As long as nothing else happened, of course.

"Mom, did you see my essay?" Xander asked as he joined her in the hallway.

Cheryl inspected her sixteen-year-old, grateful to see he still hadn't gone back to his old style of clothing. The super dramatic, "emo" —as Jade liked to call them—ones. He'd had a tough patch there for a bit, but the return of Cheryl's brother had really helped him through it.

"Last I saw it was on the table." She headed down the hall toward the kitchen. "It's not there anymore?"

Xander shook his head. "That's where I remember it being too."

"Did you ask Jade? She cleared the table for dinner."

"Yeah, but she's upset about something, and I couldn't get her to answer."

They'd reached the kitchen by then, but Xander's comment about Jade caused Cheryl to turn around again, holding on to the mental image of scrambled eggs and toast as she went to find her daughter.

Jade was a good kid—always had been—but when something upset her, it could take a long time to calm her down. Better to help her from the start instead of dealing with the aftermath.

Cheryl found her in the bathroom, digging through the top drawer of the cabinet.

"What's up, honey?"

"I can't find my new mascara, and the old stuff is so dry it's just clumping up and making a big mess."

Both kids missing something. Typical.

Cheryl started searching with Jade, but the girl's frantic motions were making it harder than it needed to be. She turned to her daughter, placed her hands on her shoulders, and said, "Sit on the toilet lid. Breathe in and out. I've got an extra tube in my bathroom if we can't find yours."

They preferred different colors of mascara, but Jade would use whatever she needed in order to avoid going without entirely.

After some digging, Cheryl found the new stuff and handed it to her daughter, then turned to find some makeup remover wipes.

Five minutes later, Jade looked great, but Cheryl's hopes for scrambled eggs and toast had disappeared.

Jade and Xander both grabbed an apple and banana, then ran out the door to catch the bus.

Cheryl watched them go, the melancholy feeling returning.

She loved her kids. More than anything. But a part of her was missing—she felt that gaping pit almost every day and had for years now. It wasn't her turn, though. Maybe someday, when the kids were older and gifting her with grandbabies. When they didn't need her constant help anymore.

With a shake of her head, Cheryl turned to grab her shoes, purse, and keys. No sense wallowing in pity when she needed to get to work.

A glance at the time on her phone showed she'd be five minutes late again. Ugh. She sent one last longing glance at the fridge, then grabbed a breakfast bar to eat in the car and stepped out of the house.

While driving, she realized she hadn't helped Xander find his essay. He hadn't mentioned it again, though, and she hoped that meant he'd found it.

Cheryl entered the cardiology department of Alpine Hospital where she worked as a receptionist. She loved the patients and her coworkers, but the job itself definitely wasn't one to write home about.

"Morning, Cheryl," Kara, the head nurse and Cheryl's future sister-in-law, said while going through some files. "How'd Xander's essay go?"

Cheryl's brother, Jack—Kara's fiancé—had helped Xander with the research portion of the essay. "It went really well. He's really blossomed now that Jack is home."

Kara nodded, turning to face Cheryl for the first time. A sympathetic expression crossed her face. "Oh, dear. Rough morning?"

Cheryl shrugged. "Same as always, actually. Jade couldn't find her mascara and was on the verge of a breakdown. We got it handled, though."

Kara chewed her lip. "Then you must have forgotten because I don't think I've ever seen you not wearing makeup."

Cheryl felt the blood drain from her face. "Did I forget to put it on?" How was that possible? It was such a huge part of her morning routine. Was she really that distracted by the idea of a warm breakfast? Dread hit her in the pit of her stomach. The dark bags under her eyes . . . There was no way she could go through a full day of work without covering those up. And her eyelashes—several of them were turning gray! She'd had no idea eyelashes could even do that. A day without makeup wasn't a day she was willing to have.

"I'm sorry, Kara, but I have to take care of this. I'll be back in twenty minutes." The first patient would be arriving in thirty minutes. Ten minutes wouldn't be enough time for Cheryl to do her morning work tasks, but this was an emergency, and she could skip lunch to get caught up.

"I'll hold down the fort," Kara called after her.

Cheryl *really* loved her coworkers.

Luckily, the hospital was only five minutes from her home in Alpine, Utah. She did a shortened version of her makeup—using one shade of eyeshadow instead of three and a cheaper eyeliner that didn't require a perfectly steady hand—but at least she looked awake and like her eyelashes were all one shade.

Kara was sitting in her chair at the reception desk when Cheryl returned, going through the schedule. "You're lucky—our first appointment just called and canceled. You have twenty extra minutes to reconcile accounts and confirm appointments." She hopped out of Cheryl's seat and gave her a hug. "What's up? Something's bothering you."

Cheryl closed her eyes, leaning into the hug. Despite how busy Kara was, she still seemed to notice everything. "It's nothing. Just a cute romance Jade and I watched last night."

Kara nodded, an understanding expression on her face. "When I went through my breakup with Ben, I actually threw away several of my favorite DVDs. *You've Got Mail, Sweet Home Alabama*—it was a bad decision and I regret it now, but just seeing them with my other movies made me angry."

Cheryl wasn't angry anymore—that feeling had passed years earlier—but still, it helped knowing Kara understood. The woman had wasted five years on a loser.

Cheryl had wasted nine years on *her* loser.

Gratitude filled her heart that she wasn't with him anymore—she still couldn't believe she'd escaped the jerk. She didn't need to make excuses to her friends and family about his frequent absences and neglect or the way he treated her and the kids.

But the melancholy . . . it was there to stay.

"It takes a while for the sadness to leave," Kara said. "And it's not just sadness from the end of the relationship —especially not in your case. Being alone, though, is tough." She gave Cheryl another hug. "You need a vacation. You have tons of time off built up. Why don't you go somewhere for the weekend?"

Cheryl shook her head. "Can't. Andrews and Emma's wedding is Friday. And with them both out of the office, things will be insane."

"True . . . but we don't have any appointments set up for while they're gone. You could easily leave."

"And do what? The kids have school. Besides, Dr. Tuttle will be here—he'll need help."

"Yeah. From me. Or Hazel. Or we could borrow someone from another department." She put her hands on Cheryl's shoulders, looking her square in the eye. "Do it. For your sanity. Without your children."

Cheryl stared at Kara, then fell into her seat. "You're kidding, right?"

"Why would I be?" Kara sat in the other receptionist chair and logged into her account. "They're old enough to be on their own for a few days. And if it's that much a concern, Jack would let them stay at his place. Or they could stay at mine."

It was tempting . . . but Cheryl hadn't ever left them. She wasn't sure *she* could handle the separation.

"If you don't do it yourself, it'll be forced on you. None of us want that."

"That's just Jack speaking," Cheryl said. Jack was a psychologist, and he'd mentioned her need for a break more than once. Cheryl always brushed him off—things were so busy at work. That wasn't all, though. Despite the fact that her coworkers were like family to her, she worried that if she took time off, they'd realize they didn't really need her.

That was silly, and she knew it. But the worry was still there. She needed this job—needed it to support her family. Her ex hadn't once paid child support. She could drag his butt to the courts over it, but what would that get her? A trailer home in Ogden that smelled like alcohol and cigarette smoke.

No thanks.

"Speaking of the wedding this weekend, where are Andrews and Emma?" she asked.

"Already out for the day."

Cheryl dropped her head to her desk. She'd missed them? "I wanted to say goodbye."

"They'll be at their own wedding, you know—you can say bye there."

"That's not the same. I won't get a chance to really talk to them."

Kara shut down the other receptionist computer and got to her feet. "I'm sorry. They were in at five this morning and left just before you got here."

"Ugh."

At least it made her feel better about the breakfast she didn't have. If she'd had time, she would have cooked it and missed them anyway.

ONCE PATIENTS STARTED ARRIVING, things got super busy, and Cheryl lost herself in her work. It wasn't until 2pm that she realized she'd missed her lunch completely. She was just standing up to take a break when Dean Harrison stepped into the lobby, followed by a young man in a suit.

"Miss Crawford," Dean Harrison started—Cheryl was surprised he knew her name—"this is Dr. Tuttle. He'll be covering for Drs. Andrews and Thomas while they're away. He needs to meet with you and the other office staff."

Dr. Tuttle nodded, his blond curls bobbing. "I had Hazel clear the schedule for our meeting. Would you let Kara and the medical assistants know I'm ready?"

Hazel, the other receptionist, got to her feet, and together, they rounded everyone up into the conference room. Cheryl turned her attention to Dr. Tuttle as he explained how things would go while Andrews and Emma were away.

Cheryl struggled with paying attention at first because it quickly became apparent that the guy was young. How was he even a doctor already? He didn't look old enough to be out of high school yet.

"We won't have any appointments—unless they're emergencies. Harrison has been pretty explicit about that. The only reason I'm here is so the ER has their required cardiologist on staff." He stood, facing the group. "Any questions?"

"When did you graduate from high school?" Kara asked.

Cheryl hid a smile. The nurse obviously had had the same thoughts. She loved how blunt her friend was.

Dr. Tuttle cleared his throat. "Six years ago."

Kara blinked. "And you're a doctor already? Holy heck, dude."

Dr. Tuttle's cheeks flushed. "I got my college degree at

the same time as my high school diploma. I always knew what I wanted—didn't see the point wasting time."

"Impressive," Cheryl said.

Dr. Tuttle answered other questions about how running the place would go, but Cheryl was distracted. What happened to her life? How did she end up as a forty-something-year-old divorcee, working as a *receptionist*? Her plan had always—as long as she could remember—been to be a stay-at-home mom who did hair on the side. To have a house full of kids with a loving husband who had a standard nine-to-five. Instead, here she was working full-time herself, raising two teenagers on her own.

Kara would tell her to give dating a try—to go out on a limb. But she'd already tried that. Her face burned as she thought of the one time she'd really exposed her feelings. Over twenty years later, she was still embarrassed about it.

What did that say about her? She'd always struggled with getting over humiliating moments, but that one—that doozy—had scarred her for life. And it hadn't even been that bad, not compared to what other girls went through. Still, she'd had a hard time moving on.

Cheryl ate a quick lunch, wishing she could take Kara up on the vacation offer. But even if there weren't any appointments, there was still a lot of stuff to get done.

Time off would have to wait.

CHAPTER 2

*L*incoln tossed his button-up on the couch of his condo and headed into the kitchen, ready to start cooking the bacon-wrapped steak he'd prepared the night before. The sun had set twenty minutes earlier, and the kitchen was dark. He flipped on all the lights, relishing in the extra-bright bulbs he'd put in recently. Working as late as he did was a decision he made—he had no one to blame but himself—but he didn't have to come home to a dark, empty condo.

Well, maybe the empty part. With the work hours he kept, he couldn't get a pet, and he for sure had no options for marriage or a girlfriend. And he was okay with that. His job literally was his life, and he loved it. He loved his patients. He loved the excitement on their faces when they took their first step after hip replacement surgery or serious car accidents or any other of the number of things that landed them in his rehab center.

He fired up his stove, tossed the steak in a cast-iron pan, and got busy preparing the vegetables. His mom would have been so proud—he rarely ate out, and the frozen meals stacked in his freezer were only there for emergencies. He refused to eat badly just because he was single, and he'd taken his mom's advice to heart. She'd told him his future wife would idolize him and worship the ground he walked on if he learned to cook well.

He'd long since come to accept he'd never get married, but the habits his mom had helped him develop at an early age had certainly kept him healthy, fit, and relatively happy.

Being single wasn't a choice he'd made—it had been made for him by a greater power. He'd actively searched for a wife for the first ten to fifteen years of his adult life. In between the duds and dead ends, he'd been in three great relationships, had proposed three times, and had received three very disappointing rejections. Each had taken a couple of years to recover from, and after the third, he'd forced himself to recognize that some people weren't meant to get married. Somehow, he'd ended up in that camp.

Did it still bother him? Only sometimes. Not tonight, though. The warm aroma of bacon-wrapped steak was enough to make him happy it was only for him. He'd enjoy every bite of it.

Lincoln sighed, recognizing the familiar lie that had become so much a part of his regular spiel.

Time for a distraction. He went to his room to retrieve the murder mystery he'd started the night before. It was a real nailbiter—just the thing to distract him until it was time to sleep. It also distracted him from the smell of his dinner long enough for the meat to finish cooking before his stomach ate itself. Things had been no busier than normal at the center, but he'd still been unable to find time to take a lunch.

It just made his dinner that much more appealing.

Too bad he didn't have anyone to share it with.

Lincoln served up the steak and veggies, then sat at his table to eat while reading.

Life really *was* good. He'd made it that way—coming to grips with his "always alone" realization, and choosing to be happy anyway.

Lemon to lemonade and all of that.

CHAPTER 3

*W*ednesday, on her way home from work, Cheryl stopped by the care facility her mom was staying in. Helen, her mom, had fallen a month or so earlier, and the break had been bad enough for her to need hip replacement surgery. Cheryl couldn't wait for her mom to be finished with all the rehab. The woman was her anchor, her rock. Having her incapacitated had been very stressful.

She knocked on her mom's door, then opened when her mom called for her to enter.

"Cheryl! How wonderful to see you. Jack was just here —you missed him by fifteen minutes."

"That's too bad. How's he doing?"

"So good. I still can't believe he and Kara are getting married."

Cheryl gave her mom a smile. "Me neither. I didn't think he'd ever settle down."

Jack had gotten restless in his profession as a psychologist and had turned to politics to help people on a broader scale. When their mom had broken her hip, he'd decided it was time to come home and settle down.

Cheryl was happy for her brother—very happy. But she wanted the same happiness for herself.

"You've been so discouraged lately, honey," Helen said.

Cheryl sighed. "Is it that obvious? I'm sorry. I'm trying not to bring it here."

"Why not?"

Cheryl gestured to her mom's hip. "You need to focus on getting better."

"You're kidding, right? I can't even begin to tell you how bored I am. I could use emotion-laden conversations to distract me."

"Oh, thank heavens. I miss our in-depth discussions."

"What's on your mind, sweetheart?"

Cheryl leaned forward. "Where to begin? Life sucks. I mean, parts of it—the love aspect. I'm so lonely again, Mom. It's like, I get to a good point in life, then something happens to remind me that I'm raising two kids on my own. I hate it."

"What happened this time?"

"Nothing big. Jade and I watched a new chick flick."

Helen gave a sad smile. "Those are bound to depress anyone who isn't in a happy relationship."

Cheryl nodded, knowing just how much her mom missed her dad. "But it was worse this time. I haven't been this discouraged in a very long time. Usually, I'm busy enough at work not to notice that I'm lonely. But not even work has been enough."

Helen glanced at the clock. "Aren't your bosses getting married tomorrow? Won't having them be gone mix things up a bit?"

Cheryl loved that Andrews and Emma had hit it off so well. "Yes, it will. That'll be different, and I'm sure it'll help." Cheryl also looked at the clock, then turned back to her mom. "Are you expecting someone?"

"Huh? Oh, yes, but not for a bit still. My physical therapist is coming soon to work with me. You can stay while I'm doing my exercises."

"You don't mind?"

"Of course not."

Cheryl leaned back in her chair. "Good." She closed her eyes for a moment.

"Is the wedding part of your discouragement?" Helen asked.

Cheryl shook her head. "No, actually, and that surprises me." She opened her eyes. "I honestly don't feel any negative emotions about that—it was all the movie."

"Well, let's see if we can distract you."

"How?"

"Who needs a distraction?" A deep voice spoke from the doorway behind Cheryl.

Cheryl's hand fluttered to her mouth, and her heart practically jumped out of her chest. A cold sweat passed over her, and she felt every ounce of blood drain from her face. She hadn't heard that voice for over twenty years, but it was as familiar to her as her own mother's voice.

Lincoln Tanner was right behind her. Cheryl closed her eyes, not wanting to see him, not wanting him to see *her*. She prayed he'd aged poorly, then immediately felt bad for having the thought.

"Cheryl does."

Cheryl felt her cheeks warm. "I'm fine, Mom."

"Oh, so you're the daughter Helen talks about all the time."

She heard him step into the room and finally opened her eyes. It was weird for her to keep them closed when she was supposed to be meeting someone.

Cheryl got to her feet, not wanting to have a reunion while she was slumped in a hospital chair. She met his gaze, her breath catching. His eyes—his face—all of it was nearly the same. His body hadn't changed an ounce. He was still tall, trim, with an easy smile. His nearly black hair was longer now, and he was letting the natural curl come out. His chocolate brown eyes twinkled, and she found herself swooning just a bit. Those eyes had been the thing that had caused her crush to develop in the first place.

Knock it off, Cheryl.

She waited a moment, expecting him to recognize her. But no recognition crossed his face. He had no clue who she was. How was that possible? Had she made that little of an impression on him? Or had she changed so much where she was no longer recognizable? She resisted the urge to look down, but she basically wore the same size as she had in high school, with a few adjustments to be made for having two children. She'd always been fairly lithe, and had struggled with gaining weight even during her pregnancies.

If not her body, then maybe her face? Had she developed so many wrinkles where she was unrecognizable?

But being in his presence again . . . It felt like someone pricked her heart with a tiny knife, twisting it slowly. Too many years had passed for her to feel the pain acutely, but not enough had passed for her to have gotten over the experience.

"Lincoln. Good to see you again."

Lincoln shook her hand, then paused. "We know each other?"

"You could say that. Though, *knew* would be the better word."

How had Cheryl not known he worked here? Oh, maybe he was a lackey—someone lower in the ranks. An aide or something. That gave her a moment of contentment. She might be a divorcee working as a receptionist, but knowing he wasn't in a great position made her feel a little better.

"I was wondering if you'd remember Dr. Lincoln," Cheryl's mom said. "When I found out he went to your junior high and high school, I was positive you'd know him."

Doctor? Ugh. The unfairness of the universe was so . . . so . . . unfair.

"You didn't tell me your daughter went to school with me," Lincoln said, pushing a strand of curls away from his eyes. Cheryl was almost hypnotized by the action. Even that much was familiar to her.

Man, she'd had it *bad* for this guy.

"I didn't? I could have sworn I did. What an odd detail to leave out."

Cheryl narrowed her eyes at her mom. There was no way she had forgotten. Cheryl had talked about nothing other than Lincoln Tanner for five years straight.

"Did we have classes together?" Lincoln asked.

"Yes. Several." She was still so affected by him and he had *no clue* who she was. So embarrassing. Not for the first time, she regretted she'd ever asked him out. At least he didn't remember that happening.

Cheryl's gaze dropped to his nametag.

Lincoln Tanner, Physical Therapist.

"Why are you calling yourself a doctor? You're a PT."

"I didn't call myself a doctor—your mom did."

"He holds a doctorate of physical therapy, dear. He *is* a doctor."

"Doctors are supposed to be surgeons." The minute the words were out of her mouth, Cheryl realized how silly she sounded. Doctors could be anything—all they needed was a PhD. Still, she refused to take it back. "And why go by your first name? What happened to your last name?"

He shrugged. "It's what the patients here all call me."

"Because your aides call you that," Helen said.

"Because my first patient did." He glanced at Cheryl, an apology in his eyes. "I'd prefer they call me Lincoln, but nicknames are hard to get rid of once people start using them."

Cheryl almost nodded before stopping herself. She wasn't giving him an inch of acceptance. But she knew what he was talking about—he'd been called Pres their entire senior year. Getting elected as student body president would do that to someone.

She'd been under the impression, even back then, that the nickname had bothered him. But he'd never done anything to get people to stop, so it obviously hadn't annoyed him enough.

"Yeah, well, you could ask them not to call you that anymore." *Ugh. What the heck, Cheryl? Why are you being so rude?* She needed to leave—she was bound to continue opening her mouth when she shouldn't.

"Honey, what's up with you today? You're not usually this crabby." Helen glanced at Lincoln. "She's not usually this crabby. I'm sorry you've found her on a bad day."

Cheryl's mouth popped open. "Mom, you know very

well what happened between Lincoln and me. Maybe I'm being crankier than usual, but trust me, it's well deserved. He isn't the wonderful person you think he is."

A confused expression crossed his face. "Something happened between us?"

Cheryl scowled. She had zero desire to hash out the past. But still—she'd wondered about that night for many years. Her life would have been so very different if he'd followed through. "*Nothing* happened. That's the problem. I asked you out for Sadie Hawkins, you said yes, but when I went to pick you up, you weren't there. Boy, did *Whitney* have fun with that."

"Whitney Dickens? The cheerleader? Wow. Now, *that's* a name I haven't heard in a long time. I hate to say it, but if she was your friend, you should have known she'd make fun of you. That girl—"

He shut his mouth, but he'd obviously been about to say more. Cheryl was tempted to ask what, but held back. She didn't want to gossip, and she especially didn't want to relive those years. Whitney had made her life a living hell.

"I'm sorry," Lincoln finally said, "but I honestly don't remember any of this. I apologize . . . for standing you up."

His tone of voice made it obvious he wasn't sure he believed she'd ever asked him out. Standing someone up hadn't been his M.O.

And that was what had hurt so much. Lincoln had been very popular, yes, but he'd also been considerate and nice. It had taken her years to get up the courage to ask him out, but she'd been so positive he'd say yes.

It never occurred to her that he'd say yes, then stand her up.

She swore he wouldn't find out how hard that had

been for her. She'd been quiet, shy, and awkward as a teenager. It normally hadn't been difficult for her to ask someone out—at least, not any worse than it was for other girls. But asking out the guy she'd crushed on for years? So incredibly hard. And having him stand her up was the most humiliating thing she'd ever experienced.

Not even her failed marriage had scarred her as much. What did that say about her? The fact that Lincoln didn't remember hurt far more than it should have, given the years that had passed since then.

Cheryl's urge to dart from the room returned, and this time, she didn't ignore it.

"I've got to go, Mom. Thanks for the chat."

She left the room, walking several steps down the hall before leaning against a wall and breathing deeply. She needed to be calmer before returning to work.

Lincoln continued talking to her mom, his voice drifting down the hall to Cheryl, and she realized she hadn't gone far enough.

"I'm really sorry about that—I wish I could remember what happened. Obviously, I owe her an apology. A more sincere one, anyway."

"Don't worry about it, Lincoln. I'm sorry she was cranky when you came."

Cheryl scowled. What happened to "*Dr.* Lincoln"?

"Even so, I could have made that less awkward." His voice muffled for a bit, and Cheryl imagined him rubbing his face. "I didn't realize this before, but you're right—I need a vacation. I'm here way too much." A grumbling sound drifted toward Cheryl. "We're always so short staffed, though."

Was that something he should be sharing with a patient? Cheryl wouldn't have. Regardless, she knew something about being short staffed. The cardiology department was finally catching up, but they'd struggled hard to meet the needs of their patients for a long while.

A vacation would be very nice. Cheryl felt herself softening to the idea because running at full speed was getting old.

CHAPTER 4

*L*incoln couldn't stop thinking about his encounter with Cheryl as he worked with his patients. Did she really ask him out? There was no way he would have stood her up. At least, he didn't think so. But if she was telling the truth—and why would she lie?—he had actually done it.

He didn't remember anything, not even her. He prided himself on having a good memory, and that really bothered him. Especially considering how attractive she was. Her eyes—solidly green and framed by the longest natural eyelashes he'd ever seen—were spectacular. And despite the fact that she was his age, her face was still smooth and youthful, only laugh lines around her eyes. Despite being angry with him, she'd carried herself with a lot of grace and elegance. Almost as if she'd been a ballerina her whole life. She had the figure for it—slight and slender—and he imagined holding her in his arms. She would tuck perfectly under his chin.

Concentrate, Lincoln. You still have work to do.

When he finally finished with his last patient, instead

of doing his final rounds, checking on each of his patients before heading home, he asked his aides to do it for him. He didn't have them do it often so this one time wouldn't be a problem. He had a mystery to solve.

Grateful he'd always been a journal writer, once he got home, he dug through his boxes of journals, pulling out the ones from high school. He'd had a lot of girlfriends and had always been loyal to them, which meant he wouldn't have said yes to Cheryl if he'd been in a relationship. That narrowed down his search considerably. And she'd said it was for Sadie Hawkins.

Lincoln wracked his brain, trying to remember when Sadie Hawkins usually took place. Was it a spring or fall dance? He Googled it, but that didn't help—people held them at different times of the year. He seemed to remember it being in the spring, though. So, sometime in the spring when he wasn't in a relationship was where he'd start.

He scanned through three years of journals, then finally found something only a couple of months before graduation. It was a small entry.

Was supposed to have a date tonight with a girl from school named Cheryl. Didn't make it. Mom and Dad were in an accident.

The next entry was a full month later.

Lincoln fell back on his heels, floored. Memories tried to overtake him, and he struggled not to follow the rabbit down various holes. His parents' accident. The stress of the following months. Him almost not graduating. Missing so much school. Tutors.

That accident . . . it had been horrible.

He straightened, going back to reading his journal to see if any mention of Cheryl cropped up again.

Got back with Brittany. Mom and Dad are still in bad shape.

Their accident was so awful. They hydroplaned on the freeway and lost control of the car. They're still in the hospital, and it's been a month. Doctors don't think either of them will be released for several months. So much damage to their bodies. Poor Mom and Dad. Brittany has helped so much. I don't know what I'd do if she weren't around.

He didn't mention Cheryl again. Lincoln wasn't sure *when* she'd asked him out as none of the previous entries mentioned it. That wasn't surprising—when he was between girlfriends, he got asked out a lot. It was a product of being student body president.

The more he thought about what happened, though, the more came back to him. He didn't remember the date until two days after it was supposed to happen, and no wonder. His parents had consumed his every thought. He'd practically lived in the hospital while waiting to see if they'd make it or not.

When he'd remembered, he'd asked Brittany to let the girl know what happened. She obviously never did—she must have forgotten. He knew she wouldn't have failed to communicate with Cheryl for petty reasons. She was one of the most charitable and compassionate girls he'd ever known.

Brittany was someone he couldn't think about without pain. She'd been one of his rejections.

Lincoln turned his thoughts back to Cheryl. He remembered the circumstances now, but he still couldn't remember *her* at all. Still on a Retrieve Memories mission, Lincoln found the box that had yearbooks in it, pulling out the one from his senior year. *What was her name back then?* Davis was her mom's last name, so he flipped to the Ds and found her there. Cheryl Davis.

Lincoln found himself half smiling at her picture,

feeling a bit of sympathy for the girl she'd been. She'd definitely changed. Her shoulders stooped forward protectively, her arms crossed in front of her. She had braces, glasses, a bit of face acne, and very frizzy hair. Most girls had frizzy hair back then, so that wasn't a big deal, but he immediately felt bad as he realized why he hadn't remembered her. Her body language practically begged people to ignore or overlook her. He doubted they'd even spoke before she'd asked him out.

He couldn't imagine how hard it would have been for her to get up the nerve to approach him. That poor girl. What a way to ruin someone's life. She was obviously still upset at him, despite more than twenty years having passed since their senior year.

Lincoln sighed, setting the books aside and leaning against the wall of his closet. He'd probably never see her again, but he hoped if he did, he'd be able to smooth things over. It killed him to think of the pain she'd experienced because of him. Never mind the fact that he'd been going through the worst trial of his life during that time—he wasn't a flake or a jerk, and he hated knowing someone out there was upset with him.

Especially someone as vulnerable as she'd been.

Dang it. He needed a shower to clear his mind. Then he needed a great dinner and another murder mystery.

CHAPTER 5

*C*heryl really struggled with concentrating at work Thursday. She couldn't help but feel grateful she and Lincoln hadn't tried to catch up on each other's lives. What did she have to show for herself? He'd obviously accomplished much more than she had.

Her marriage to her ex had stopped her beauty school dreams. He'd been very opposed to it and had refused to pay. Her mom had warned her multiple times. "What if something happens to your husband? Cheryl, you need to have a contingency plan. Something in place that could keep you and your kids fed."

Cheryl had seen the wisdom in it, and her parents would probably have offered to help pay for it, but her pride had prevented her from asking for help. That, and her parents hadn't been well off either.

Now, she had no time to go to school or receive training to become something more than a receptionist. She was locked in place—no forward movement possible until her kids were older and on their own.

That was at least six years away. Could she last that long?

Cheryl updated another patient's file, feeling herself entering a depressive cycle. It was as if she was suffocating, like the world around her was numb, mute.

She pushed through her work, only talking to people when she had to. When Kara invited her to go out for ice cream, Cheryl turned her down. The last thing she wanted was to be social.

Kara folded her arms, standing in front of Cheryl as she grabbed her purse and tried to leave. "Cheryl, you *never* say no to ice cream. What's going on?"

Cheryl slumped back into her seat. There was no point in denying that something had happened—Kara would pester her until she relented and told the story anyway. "My mom's physical therapist is a guy I had a crush on for over five years when I was a teenager."

Kara's eyes widened. "Helen's therapist is *Lincoln*?"

Cheryl blinked. "I told you about him?"

"Yeah, when I went through my breakup with Ben. You were trying to cheer me up."

Cheryl half laughed. "Did it help?"

"It definitely distracted me. I was so mad at him for you. 'Shy girl asks out popular guy, gets stood up, and is tortured for months by snobbish teenager.' So awful. It helped me shift some of my anger from Ben to Lincoln."

"I can't believe you remember his name."

"Of course I do. I like the name Lincoln." Kara sighed, then her expression softened. "So, what happened? Did he apologize? Or was he a jerk?"

Cheryl shook her head. "He didn't even remember I'd asked him on a date. He probably thought I was lying, if his expression of 'you're crazy' was to be believed."

"Oh, Cheryl, I'm so sorry. Did you strangle him? Scalp him? Leap across the room at him with a knife?"

"Kara! Sheesh. He hurt me, yes, but I never once wanted to murder him over it. Geez."

Kara laughed. "What did your mom do?"

"Ugh. She apologized to him for me being cranky."

Kara's mouth popped open. "You're *kidding*. Where's the loyalty, Mom?"

"Seriously."

"Do you want to go buy a bunch of dishes from Deseret Industries and smash them in a parking lot somewhere? Someone wise once told me about that. She called it cheap therapy. We'd clean up after, promise."

Cheryl laughed. She was the one who'd suggested Kara do that after her relationship with Ben ended. "No, I don't think so. I'd rather have a quiet evening."

"I understand." Kara gave Cheryl a concerned expression. "Really, though. Is there anything I can do for you?"

"Be my fairy godmother and transform me into something I'm not?" Cheryl motioned to her body. "This isn't exactly what I envisioned him seeing if we were ever in the same room again."

Kara's mouth popped open. "What are you talking about? You're beautiful. You've aged gracefully—most women can't say the same. And you're in fantastic shape."

Cheryl appreciated the compliment but knew if Kara saw her in a swimming suit she'd change her mind. She was thin, yes, but the extra folds of skin from being pregnant had never gone away. And her stretch marks. Ugh. "He didn't even send a second glance my way." Exactly the same as high school. Always invisible.

"That's his fault. Not yours. Besides, I'm sure he doesn't look very good now."

Cheryl groaned, dropping her face into her hands. "That's the awful part. He looks even *better*. I've always been a sucker for men with hair graying at their temples."

"Like Dean Harrison?"

Cheryl jerked up to look at Kara. "What? Ew. No. He is *not* my type."

"Just saying. He's got graying hair at the temples. And I'm sure we could find other men like that too, if that's your only criteria."

Cheryl shook her head. "No. No men. I need to bury myself in my work." And her kids' homework. And their extracurricular activities. There was a lot of driving back and forth to do.

Kara raised an eyebrow. "Darling, you need to bury yourself in a *vacation*. Have you given what I said yesterday any thought?"

"Yup, I have." Cheryl was pleased with herself for having an answer so quickly. "The kids and I just went to Disneyland." She didn't know why she hadn't remembered that—it had only been a couple of months ago.

Kara scoffed. "How relaxing was that for you?"

Huh. Good point. No wonder she hadn't remembered. "I can't very well go on a vacation alone, now, can I?"

"Why not?" Kara pulled out her phone and sent a text, then tucked the device away. "Just think about it, okay?"

Cheryl promised she would, but she doubted anything would come of it.

≈

Not twenty minutes later, Cheryl got a call from her mom. She gripped the phone, holding it hard against her ear. The last time her mom had called instead of texted, she'd been in a lot of pain.

"Mom! Are you okay?"

"Of course I am. I need you to come by as soon as you can, though."

"What's going on?"

"It's an emergency, but not a medical one."

"You're not going to make me be in the same room with Lincoln Tanner again, are you? I wish you'd warned me yesterday that was going to happen."

"No, dear, I'm not. I'm sorry about that—I know it was really awkward for you both."

Cheryl snorted. "Awkward for him? I'll say—he couldn't even remember who I was."

"Mmhmm. When are you coming?"

"I'll be there for my lunch."

"So, in an hour?"

Cheryl looked at the time on her computer. "About forty-five minutes."

Helen gave an excited squeal. "Perfect. See you soon."

Cheryl couldn't help but chuckle when she put her phone back in her purse. Her mom used to get excited like that on a regular basis, but her fall, then the subsequent surgery—and all the complications that had come with that—had tampered her bright spirit for a while. It was good to hear that she was getting her spark back.

The time until her lunch break went quickly, and Cheryl was soon on her way to the rehab center. As she entered the building, she saw Lincoln's name on the sign and wished she'd paid closer attention to it the day before or even while she'd been helping get her mom settled in after the surgery. It showed just how stressed she'd been recently that she hadn't noticed.

Cheryl walked quickly toward her mom's room, glancing around as she did and vowing to pretend not to see Lincoln if he was there—all while praying he wouldn't be.

She stepped into her mom's room with a sigh of relief and sat in her usual chair, glad to see the light in her mom's eyes that she'd heard on the phone. Helen's face practically glowed, she was so excited.

"What's up, Mom?"

"Kara and I have been conniving all day. You're going on a vacation. To Hawaii."

"Wait, what? How?" Cheryl's thoughts stumbled all over themselves. "No, I'm not. I can't go now—I haven't gotten work off, and the kids need me to help with their homework and activities and everything."

"It's all been taken care of. Kara arranged for everything with the temp doctor, and Xander and Jade are going to stay with Jack. His practice here is new enough where he can shuttle them back and forth to everything without causing a problem for his own patients. And the fact that he lives here in Alpine means the kids can take the bus to and from school still."

Cheryl's brain was still going a million miles a second. She couldn't just drop everything and fly to an island in the middle of the ocean. "I can't afford to go to Hawaii."

"Nope."

"And neither can you."

"Nope."

"Then how is this getting paid for?"

"Remember Susan and Tom? Dad's friends at the university?"

Cheryl nodded. Her dad had taught in Hilo for several years. Tom was a colleague there, and Cheryl had met him and Susan multiple times when they'd come to the mainland. "Of course."

"They have a vacation rental on the other side of the island. They've offered it to me multiple times, and they're thrilled to have you stay there for a week while you relax."

"A *week*?" That was much longer than she'd expected.

"Anything less and it wouldn't be worth the travel days. By the time you get caught up from a full day of flying, you'd be needing to head back home. So Kara and I arranged for you to stay there for a week."

"But who's paying for the plane ticket?"

"Jack is. Kind of. He has a ton of miles he hasn't used."

"He'll need them for his honeymoon."

"Not all of them." Helen leaned forward. "Cheryl, honey, everything has already fallen into place. The only thing you'll need to do is replace whatever food you eat while you're there, plus pay for a rental car and gas."

"Replace the food I eat?"

Helen nodded. "Susan keeps the kitchen well stocked."

"And pay for a car?"

Helen nodded again. "It won't be too much—only a couple hundred." She leaned over and grabbed a piece of paper, handing it to Cheryl. "Everything's right here."

Cheryl stared at the paper. It had flight and rental car info on it, complete with confirmation numbers. "It's already been paid for—all of it?"

"Yes."

Tears filled Cheryl's eyes. "I'm going to Hawaii?"

Helen smiled at her. "Yes. Right after Emma's wedding tomorrow."

The tears spilled over, and relief flooded Cheryl's system. She needed a vacation—desperately. She knew she did.

And just like that, she was getting one.

CHAPTER 6

*L*incoln entered the break room, chatting on the phone with his friend as he did so. Their conversation was long overdue, but their schedules made it difficult to get in touch. Mark had three kids now and his wife was expecting a fourth. They lived far enough away where talking during Lincoln's lunch was necessary.

He pulled out his wallet, removing a sheet of googly eyes, then stepped to the fridge, a grin stealing across his face.

"How is the center going?" Mark asked.

"Pretty great. I've got the best staff right now—they've been very patient with me."

Mark chuckled. "You still pulling pranks on them?"

Lincoln grinned again as he removed several of the googly eye stickers, attaching them to Kati's lunch and a few other things in the fridge. Kati would get a kick out of it. After she got over her shock, anyway. She'd been his assistant for several years and could easily take any teasing he sent her way.

"Does a dog bark?"

"How are they responding?"

Lincoln put the sheet of eyes back into his wallet, returning it to his front pocket. "Exactly as they should." He tried to hire people who didn't mind some ribbing and mild pranks. It hadn't backfired yet, and he didn't expect it ever would. He read people fairly well and could usually tell in the first interview if someone would handle his personality or not.

"Excellent. Did I tell you about Kaden's last football practice?"

"I don't think so."

Lincoln warmed up his food, listening as Mark jumped into a hilarious story about his nine-year-old. The pang of sadness that hit Lincoln's chest wasn't unexpected, but it still frustrated him. He'd worked so hard to tuck away all of the negative emotions over marriage and family.

He was happy for Mark—very happy. And Mark wasn't ever insensitive to Lincoln. In fact, if they'd been together, he would have recognized Lincoln's melancholy immediately. Mark was a rarity—very in-tune with people's feelings. There was a reason he'd become a family counselor. He could read emotions easier than a bat could see in the dark.

Still, it wasn't fair to him to have to hold back for Lincoln's sake.

Someone knocked on the door jamb to the lunch room, and Lincoln glanced up. His older brother, Joshua, stood there. Lincoln ended the call with Mark, and gave his brother a hug.

"Joshua!" Lincoln said. "What are you doing here?"

Joshua shrugged. "Just wanted to come hang out for a

bit. Work is slow, and I figured you could use a break from the insanity here."

Lincoln nodded. "That would be nice."

They made small talk while Lincoln scarfed down his food. He had a new patient coming later that day, and he needed to make sure everything would be handled before she arrived.

"Why is work slow?" Lincoln asked when he'd finished eating.

"The usual—newest therapist at the facility, and they don't have enough patients coming in to shovel new ones on me yet."

Lincoln understood that. He hadn't been in the same position for a while, but it had been tedious in the beginning of his career.

Joshua had been in the military for several years before deciding to become a physical therapist, like his younger brother. He'd worked at several facilities during the last ten years before finding the current one, and he seemed to really enjoy it there. But, as he said, being new could be boring.

"What are you going to do in the meantime?"

Joshua cleared his throat louder than needed, and Kati entered the room. "That's where I come in," she said.

Lincoln raised his eyebrow. The throat clearing had obviously been her sign to enter. "You'd better not be trying to quit, Kati."

She laughed. "You kidding? Joshua couldn't pay me well enough."

"Correct," Joshua said, and Lincoln and Kati both laughed.

"But we've been talking," she said. "Helen—you know, your patient—mentioned knowing a married couple in

Hawaii who own a vacation rental. Part of it is under construction, so they can't officially rent it out. They told Helen that if she knows someone who doesn't mind dust and paint cans, they'd let them stay for free and to point them in their direction."

Lincoln washed his plate in the sink. "I still don't see what that has to do with you and Joshua. Are you planning on going together?"

"Becca and I are busy," Joshua said, "And Kati and her husband aren't interested."

Lincoln shrugged. "And . . .?"

"We think *you* should go," Kati said. "I've been working here for nine years, and you still haven't taken a vacation. You've only missed one day of work, and that was six years ago."

"The thing is," Joshua said, "all work and no play makes Johnny a cranky boy."

"I thought it was 'dull boy,'" Lincoln said.

A vacation would be nice, but now was not the time to take one. He had far too many things on his plate.

"*You* probably haven't noticed it, but your *employees* have," Kati said. "You're very stressed out. You spend sixteen hours a day here, and it's starting to show."

Lincoln scowled, folding his arms. "In what way?"

"When was the last time you pulled a prank on someone?"

Lincoln held a straight face—the last time had been only minutes before Kati entered the room. But before that? He wracked his brain, trying to remember, and was astonished to find that Kati was right—it had been so long since the last practical joke that he didn't even know when it had happened.

Kati nodded. "My point exactly. You're stretched so

thin here that something any day now is going to push you over the edge, and your life will implode." She motioned to herself and Joshua. "That's where we come in."

Even the thought of half a day away made Lincoln's chest tighten. No way was he leaving, not while things were going so well. He didn't want to curse himself and return to a disaster.

"Let me guess," he said to Kati, "you're going to take over working with patients for me?"

Kati scoffed. "As if. No, I'm going to clear your schedule as much as possible, and have Joshua step in until you return."

She wasn't even finished talking and Joshua was already nodding. Lincoln turned to him. "And this is okay with you?"

Joshua dropped his head back and groaned. "I'm soooooo boooooored." He clasped his hands in front of him and said, "Pleeease help me out."

Lincoln chuckled. Joshua *had* been complaining a lot lately about his lack of workload.

"I have a new patient coming today," he said, knowing that wouldn't stop the two determined adults in front of him. Should he go on a vacation? He hadn't ever been to Hawaii.

Joshua nodded. "We know. We're ready."

Shifting a patient to an entirely different facility wasn't an easy feat. It required a lot of calls to insurance and juggling all sorts of schedules and availabilities. That wasn't something Lincoln had planned to spend his precious time doing.

"I've already started the initial calls," Kati said in an attempt to strengthen her argument. It made Lincoln wonder if she could read his mind. "Just to get the ball rolling." She stepped in front of him and put her hands on his arms. "Please, Lincoln. This place is running excellently, and between your staff and Joshua, it'll continue to do so while you take a much-deserved break. You need this vacation. Like a flower needs the sun. Like the earth needs rain. Like a car needs power. Like grass needs water. Like tires need air. Like—"

Lincoln laughed. "All right, I get it. I'll think about it."

She shook her head. "No, you won't *think* about it. You're *doing* it."

Joshua stepped up to Lincoln too, and he felt like a cornered animal. "I promise I'll take good care of your patients. I know you trust me—it'll be fine."

Lincoln did trust Joshua. He knew his brother's work ethic was intense—the man wouldn't let anything fall through the cracks. Still, though . . .

"Let me give it some thought for at least a few minutes, then. I promise I'll make a decision quickly." He just needed to ponder it over for a bit—make sure they really *did* have all the pieces of the puzzle considered and in place.

The hardest part about running a rehab center was taking care of the patients. If Kati and Joshua already had a plan for all of that, he really didn't have much to do.

But a vacation? To Hawaii?

He wasn't sure about that.

Kati watched him as he processed things, then glanced at Joshua. "Okay, we'll give you ten minutes. Hope that's enough time."

Before Lincoln could complain, they stepped out of the room. *Ten minutes?* That definitely was *not* enough time.

Still, he promise he'd consider it, and he would do just that.

Going on vacation. Not something he ever imagined he'd do alone. But Kati was right . . . he really *did* need the break.

What did he have to lose? Nothing, really. But he still struggled with making the decision. Leaving his patients felt like a betrayal.

Knowing he wouldn't be able to decide until he paced his halls, he walked out of the lunch room, passing Kati and Joshua in the hall, and started walking, hands in his pockets.

Would it really be a betrayal? No—he knew it wouldn't be. At least, logically, he understood that. But emotionally, it still felt wrong.

Would it ever feel right, though? Would there ever come a time where he didn't panic at the thought of leaving? Would he ever feel like he was ready for time away?

Kati was right about one thing—he hadn't taken any time off, except for that one day. Ten years was a very, very long time not to have a break.

Was she also right about him being on the verge of a burnout? He wasn't sure, but as he searched his feelings, he realized he was absolutely exhausted. To the core. If that wasn't a sign that he needed a break, he didn't know what would be.

His thoughts flitted back to his patients. They were the reason he pushed himself so hard. They were worth it, of course. Could he leave them, though?

Helen was the one who had all the connections. Before even realizing he'd made the decision to do so, Lincoln found himself walking toward her room.

$\approx$

HELEN GRINNED. "I'm so glad you're considering it. This is a once-in-lifetime opportunity, and I really do feel like you should take it."

"Well, *of course* you do—it was partially your idea."

She leaned forward into a stretch he'd shown her, and sent him a stern expression. "Lincoln Tanner, if you don't take a vacation soon, you will start to unravel. I don't know when—it might be a week from now or a month or even a year, but unravel you will. I've been here for two weeks, and I happen to be your most observant patient."

He chuckled. Helen was also his favorite patient.

"I didn't say that to be funny. The lines around your eyes are deepening. The pressure you're under is visible to someone who pays attention. You need to pass off control of this facility to your brother's capable hands while you step out from under its weight and take some time for yourself."

Lincoln ran a hand over his eyes, feeling her words to the core. He felt that weight now. She wasn't exaggerating about anything she'd said—she really *was* more observant than most of his patients. And the fact that she was willing to go to bat for him really touched him.

"None of my previous patients have ever done something like this for me." He waved a hand in the air. "Oh, several have mentioned it, but none have actually gone to the effort of finding a place for me to stay."

Helen took his hand and gave it a squeeze. "You need it."

"I know." He took in a deep breath, let it out slowly, then said, "And I'm looking forward to it."

Helen's eyes widened, and she froze, staring at him. "So you're going?"

He shrugged. "Doesn't seem like I have much of a choice, does it?"

She glowered at him. "You *always* have a choice."

Lincoln took a seat next to her bed and leaned forward, clasping his hands, his gaze not leaving her face. "Deep down, I know you're right about burnout. I'm passionate about my job, and being here brings me so much happiness. But I've been go-go-going for so many years that if I don't *choose* to take a break now, I might not be able to choose later."

Helen reached over and gave his hand another squeeze. "So much wisdom for someone so young."

He chuckled. "I'm not that much younger than you."

She frowned at him. "Honey, I'm old enough to be your mother."

Lincoln laughed again and got to his feet. "Guess I'd better go let Kati and Joshua know."

"Don't need to."

"What do you mean?"

A sneaky grin crossed Helen's face, and she reached to her bedside table and picked up a piece of paper. "Everything's already been put into place. Kati, Joshua, and I arranged it. All we needed was your go-ahead on the facility stuff, but the plane tickets have already been purchased."

Lincoln felt like the wind had been knocked out of him briefly, but then he grinned. "You conniving, evil people."

"Conniving, yes. Evil, no. People who are truly evil don't care for anyone but themselves. This was an act of love." She put the paper in his hand. "I'd love to get out of this place as soon as possible, and if you don't take that break, you might not be around when I need to be dispatched. Getting assigned to someone who doesn't know your system might mean I'd be here for an extra week or two, and that's totally unacceptable." She tapped her cheek. "Maybe that means I really *am* evil."

Lincoln chuckled. "Oh, you aren't. I was kidding about that." He glanced down at the paper in his hand. "When does my flight leave? And where do I send money?"

"The flights were pretty cheap—we can figure that out when you get back. The vacation rental didn't cost anything, as you already know. Maybe you remember me saying I used to live in Hawaii? I still have a lot of friends there who were willing to help out. You'll just cover the cost of the rental car, gas, and food."

"I've never been on a vacation alone before, you know."

A twinkle entered Helen's eyes. "Maybe you won't find yourself so alone when you get there. Hawaii is the city of love, after all."

Lincoln chuckled. "Hawaii isn't a city—it's a state—and *Paris* is the city of love."

Helen waved him off. "Tomatoes, tomatoes. Potatoes, potatoes. Still, I'm sure you'll make memories. Go enjoy yourself."

Lincoln promised he would. He felt like he should give her a hug or something, but resisted, unsure how she'd feel about that. Instead, he patted her hand. "Thank you, Helen."

She beamed up at him. "You're welcome."

Lincoln stepped out of her room, feeling lighter than he had in years. Knowing he wouldn't be in charge—that the place wouldn't collapse if he weren't there every second of every day—brought so much air and relief to him that he felt lightheaded.

The timing couldn't have been more perfect—he didn't have any meetings, and aside from the new patient who was going to be staying at Joshua's facility instead, he wasn't expecting anyone new.

As he was nearing his office, he saw his brother, Joshua, approaching.

"Lincoln, there you are. Did you make your decision?"

Lincoln gave his older brother a tight hug. "Thank you for arranging all of this. I really appreciate it."

"Does that mean it's a yes? You're going?"

"I guess I am."

Joshua grinned. "Right on. Oh, and *Kati* arranged everything. I'm only providing the manpower."

Lincoln blinked. "She said she'd only just started making preliminary calls."

Joshua grinned. "Everything's been done already—she knew we'd be able to convince you." He wagged a finger at Lincoln as the two of them walked to Lincoln's office. "You of all people should never underestimate a determined employee." A serious expression crossed his face. "Your people here really care for you, Lincoln."

Lincoln sensed the underlying sentiment. Joshua hoped he'd get to that point in his own place. Lincoln put a hand on his brother's shoulder. "You'll get there, I promise. Especially if these arrangements will be bringing people to your facility."

Normally, the thought that he'd be losing patients to a competitor would have given him anxiety, but his brother was different. Joshua might have been older than Lincoln, but Lincoln still felt protective of him. An itch to make sure all the people he loved were taken care of had developed around the time of his parents' accident and it hadn't gone away.

"Thank you." Joshua looked at his watch. "You have three hours to make your flight—you need to get going. Talk fast as you update me on your patients."

"*Three hours?*" Lincoln glanced at his schedule. Joshua wasn't kidding. Boy, they'd cut that close! What would have happened if he'd turned down the vacation offer? Helen would undoubtedly have lost the money from the flights.

Lincoln quickly went over the schedule, patients, and their various needs with his brother. He finished, then gave his brother another hug before heading home to pack his clothes.

He was going to have a fantastic time, even if alone.

CHAPTER 7

*C*heryl had expected to be sad about missing Emma's reception, but the more she thought about it, the more she realized just how relieved she was to have a legit excuse not to be there. When it came to Hawaii or a reminder that she wasn't happily married—yeah, Hawaii won hands down.

The flight from Salt Lake City to Seattle was over quickly. She spent the whole time grinning out the window, watching the clouds, countryside, and mountains pass below. The roar of the wind and engines wasn't nearly as loud as the constant chatter of teenagers, patients, and coworkers back home that hadn't followed her. She had no responsibilities and no conversations to take part in unless she wanted to. And because she didn't have to *or* want to, she didn't even say hi to the woman sitting next to her.

The woman didn't seem to mind.

How long had it been since Cheryl had allowed herself to just be? Silent, alone, quiet? She'd always been introspective, and having people constantly around her had worn her down over the years. She loved her children, yes, but she was now realizing how close she'd come to a breakdown.

They would all grow from this vacation—Xander and Jade would have an opportunity to be more independent, to feel like their mom wasn't hanging over every assignment and decision, and Cheryl would be forced to cut the apron strings just a bit.

She found herself looking forward to it.

The flight from Seattle to the big island was long and tedious. After she got over the excitement that she was leaving the continental United States for the first time in her life and was flying above a vast, deep ocean, hunger settled into the pit of her stomach and boredom etched its way into her brain. She ate her peanuts and ginger cookies and contented herself with watching several movies, turning up the volume so it covered the noise of flying.

The pilot interrupted *Legally Blonde* to announce their descent, and not wanting to miss anything as they approached the island, Cheryl tucked her earbuds away and turned to the window. Excited bubbles erupted in her stomach. She was almost there!

The plane turned to the left, and Cheryl was greeted by one of the most beautiful sunsets she'd ever seen. The whole sky was rosy gold, turning the ocean into a deep pinkish orange. As the sun dipped below the water, the colors became even more vibrant, and the dark volcanic rock that covered the island started looking maroon. Cheryl's eyes widened as she realized she didn't see any green anywhere. *Everything* was covered in the lava rock. Even the runway was black. This was not what she'd expected. Pictures of Hawaii always depicted lush greenery.

She couldn't wait to find other discrepancies between her expectations and reality.

The humidity encompassed her entire body the moment she left the plane. It was lovely—thick and heavy, like a comforter that had just come from the dryer.

With a grin on her face, Cheryl exited the airport, then made her way to the rental car area. They gave her a convertible, and she had to conceal a squeal. Boy, she couldn't wait to drive that thing!

The sun had long set by the time she got on the road. She settled in for the forty-minute drive to Captain Cook, stopping at Walmart on the way for some diet Dr Pepper and a few snacks. Just in case—she didn't know what she'd find when she arrived at the house.

Cheryl's parents had moved to Hawaii not long after she'd gotten married. Her husband hadn't made much money, and paying for food for the kids was always her top priority. A trip to Hawaii had been something she'd longed for, but had known not to hope for. She was too realistic to expect it to happen. Her father's professor salary wasn't enough for him to fly more than one person out at a time. There was no way she'd leave her kids with her husband just so she could go on vacation.

By the time she'd divorced him and the kids were old enough for her to leave them with someone else, her dad had retired and returned to the mainland.

Cheryl pulled up at the rental. It shared a driveway with another house, and she had to do some finagling to get around another car and to her spot.

She noticed immediately that the house had been built on stilts and was much taller than she'd expected. She climbed the stairs to the front door, keyed in a code, and let herself in. From what her mom had told her, she'd be staying in the upstairs, so she took the stairs to her left and headed up there, flipping on lights.

The main area was large and open, with high vaulted ceilings. A kitchen was at the back of the room, and she crossed to explore it. She'd eaten some of the snacks on the drive, but she needed solid food.

Cheryl dug around until she found some bread—in an airtight tupperware with a note on top that said KEEP ME SHUT!—and made herself a peanut butter sandwich, which she ate with a glass of milk and some string cheese from the fridge.

A note on the table welcomed her to the rental and gave information on food, the washer and dryer—which were located outside, interestingly enough—and where she could find extra sheets and towels.

Cheryl explored the rest of the areas of the house designated for her. They included an office, a bathroom, and a very large master bedroom, complete with a sitting area and four-poster bed.

She took one look at that bed and decided that sleep was a great idea, despite it only being nine. Cheryl changed into pajamas, turned off the lights, and dove into the sheets.

Sleep came immediately.

SHE SLEPT for twelve hours straight, waking up only because she'd gotten too hot. She rolled to a sitting position and grabbed her phone, blinking the sleep from her eyes, not surprised to see she had several missed calls and multiple text messages.

None of them were emergencies, just Xander and

Jade wondering how Hawaii was so far. She sent both of them texts, letting them know she would call later. She would have called them now, but they were in school and wouldn't be able to talk.

Excitement spread over Cheryl—there was a beach nearby and she'd die if she didn't get there as soon as possible, even before eating breakfast. She wasn't hungry, anyway.

Cheryl dressed quickly, pulled her hair into a messy bun, brushed her teeth, then headed out. She opened Google Maps on her phone and zoomed into her location, trying to figure out the easiest way to the shore. As it turned out, she was only about a block away, and a walk would be super easy.

Once there, Cheryl sat on a large rock—volcanic, of course—and breathed in deeply. The salty, humid air tickled her nose, and the breeze coming off the ocean teased wisps of hair from her messy bun.

It was absolutely perfect.

She relaxed for an hour, relishing the sound of the waves crashing into the rocks not ten feet away. But soon her stomach began grumbling, propelling her to her feet and back to the house.

She paused when she entered the front door. The door opposite her—which she assumed led to a downstairs apartment—was open. Had it been when she'd left? She couldn't remember, but she didn't think so. Was someone staying in the basement? Why hadn't anyone informed her she wouldn't be alone in the house? And where was that person now? Had they forgotten to shut their door?

Cheryl peered through the opening, holding her breath. "Hello?" she called softly.

No one answered, and instead of calling louder, she

pulled the door almost shut, stepping away and starting up the stairs quietly. She was almost to the top when she heard the microwave door in *her* kitchen shutting and several buttons on it getting pushed.

Someone was in her apartment.

Cheryl dropped quietly to the top stair, then peered around the half wall that separated the stairs from the living area. A shirtless man stood in front of the microwave, wearing flannel pants.

Cheryl's jaw dropped when she recognized who it was. *Lincoln?* What was *he* doing here?

He turned to the table that separated them, staring at a phone in his hand, and she caught sight of his chest and abs. Holy cow, the man was doing well for himself. He definitely hadn't let himself go.

As if he could feel eyes on him, Lincoln looked up and met her gaze.

His face went pale, and Cheryl felt hers burn.

"What are you doing here?" He stepped around the kitchen table toward her, and she scrambled to her feet, coming fully into the living room.

"What do you mean, what am *I* doing here? What are *you* doing here?"

"I'm on vacation," he said.

"So am I." She scowled at him, then shook her head. "*Mom.*"

"Helen is behind this, isn't she." His non-question made it obvious he'd figured it out as well.

"She has to be. She's the one who arranged this trip for me."

He frowned, tucking his phone into the pocket of his pajama pants. Cheryl blinked, noticing the pattern on them for the first time. Calvin and Hobbes. That fit him.

And so did they—nicely too. The man hadn't neglected leg day. He'd always been well-built, but being that way in his forties was so . . . so unfair. Not only did it do weird things to her insides, it made her feel even more frumpy.

"She arranged everything for me too," he was saying.

Cheryl couldn't believe her mother would do something like that. It was inconsiderate and inappropriate. How to handle it, though, now that it had happened? She couldn't very well ask him to go back home. Not after what it took to get there in the first place. Still, though . . . "You're not staying in the same house as me."

"Technically, I'm using the basement apartment."

"What are you doing up here, then?"

He motioned to the microwave. "Warming up a burrito."

For breakfast? Cheryl's stomach turned at the thought. "I can see that. My point is, why use the upstairs kitchen if there's one in the basement?"

"It's under construction. Your mom said it was why they are letting me stay for free."

Cheryl shook her head, closing her eyes. This was too much—way too much. "I can't deal with this. You need to leave."

"Yes, I agree that would be best." He turned to the microwave and pulled out his burrito, and Cheryl had a moment to pretend not to be staring at him again. She felt a familiar melancholy flood over her—to think, if he hadn't stood her up, he would be hers.

As if. The chances they'd have hit it off on that one date were incredibly slim. She'd had a lot of time to feel embarrassed for even asking him out in the first place.

ANDREA KATE PEARSON

Guys like him didn't end up with girls like her. Square peg, round hole.

Lincoln glanced up, and Cheryl was grateful her eyes had drifted while she'd been lost in thought. Instead of staring at his beautiful body, she was gazing at the wall behind him.

"Cheryl . . . I remembered what happened when you asked me out, and I'm sorry about standing you up—I really am."

He looked like he wanted to sit down and have a heart-to-heart, but Cheryl couldn't handle that right then. Nerves at being in his presence made her stomach roil, and more than anything, she needed to feel like her surroundings were a sanctuary again.

Yes, she'd hear him out eventually, but what if his story ended up hurting her even more? She wanted to be better prepared before having that conversation.

"Thank you for apologizing. I'm sure you had a good reason." She snorted inwardly. *Not likely*. "I hope you'll understand, but I really just need to be alone right now." To process everything that had happened—to figure out how to handle what felt like an enormous breach of trust on her mom's part.

Not waiting to see what Lincoln did, Cheryl stepped across the living room and entered her bedroom, shutting the door.

She couldn't believe her mom would put in this much work just to get her and Lincoln in the same space again. Wouldn't it have been easier to corner them back in her room? Why go to all the effort?

Cheryl stood near the four-poster bed, shaking from shock and countless other emotions. There were so many flowing through her that she couldn't decipher between them at first. The ones that eventually pulled to the top, though, were shock and anger. But also betrayal. Why would her mom do this to her? She *knew* how hard it had been for Cheryl to see Lincoln again! Ugh.

Cheryl grabbed her phone and called her mom.

"Hello, dear! How's Hawaii?"

"It would have been a whole lot better without a certain prank getting pulled on me."

"What prank would that be? You can't possibly be referring to Lincoln. Honey, that wasn't a prank. You both needed vacations. I knew someone who had a vacation rental. I figured why not knock out two birds with one stone?"

"Stop acting innocent. You wanted me under the same roof with him, admit it."

"Okay, fine. He's a lovely man. Don't you think you've been hurting long enough now? It's time you two had a second chance."

Cheryl sighed, slumping on the bed. Yes, she'd definitely been hurting for a long time, but the way her mom had gone about helping her was . . . it was ridiculous. Her mother was nothing, if not determined.

She was about to voice her thoughts when the floor vibrated for several seconds. Cheryl gripped her phone, holding it tight against her face. "Mom, I think we just had an earthquake."

Helen was silent for a moment. "It's an island. They have earthquakes all the time, right?"

"Maybe. I'm not sure." Didn't her mom remember from when she'd lived there?

"It wasn't very strong, was it?"

"No, not strong at all." Cheryl knew that—nothing had fallen or even really moved. Still, it was the first earthquake she'd ever felt, and it had spiked her adrenaline. She couldn't release her hold on her phone if she wanted to, and cold sweats washed over her.

"I'll pray nothing else happens there," Helen said.

Cheryl wasn't surprised that her mother didn't sound even an ounce worried. The woman was tougher than nails.

"Anyway," Helen continued. "Sorry for everything, but a mother can try, right? All I know is he is one of the best professionals I've ever worked with. And when I found out who he was, I figured it was meant to be. I mean, what are the odds he would be here, in Alpine? And further, what are the odds he'd be the guy who runs the rehab center I'm staying in? These things aren't coincidence, sweetie."

Cheryl heard the front door open and close and stepped to the window, watching as a now-fully-dressed Lincoln put a suitcase in his car, then went back inside the house.

"Well, he's leaving now."

"Oh, Cheryl, did you really make him go away?"

"Of course, Mom. The kitchen downstairs is under construction. It's not appropriate for us to stay in the same house."

"It's only inappropriate if you're sleeping in the same bed, dear."

Cheryl felt her face burn as an image of her in the same bed with a shirtless Lincoln entered her mind. "Mom! I can't believe you said that."

Helen chuckled, then sighed dramatically. "Well, enjoy your time in Hawaii, anyway."

"Me kicking him out isn't the end of the world. I'm still in Hawaii. He's still in Hawaii. We're getting the vacation you wanted us to have."

58

Helen sighed again, more sincerely this time. "But not together, and that was what I was truly hoping for."

Cheryl didn't doubt it—the woman had gone to serious lengths to get them together. "Bye, Mom. Love you."

"I love you too."

Cheryl put her phone down. Her nerves were still on edge from the shock of seeing Lincoln in her space, followed by that little earthquake.

She heard Lincoln leave the house again, and again, she went to watch from the window as he hopped in the car, turned it on, and pulled out of the driveway.

He'd only been gone for maybe a minute when another earthquake hit—this one much stronger. Cheryl dashed across the room and slid under the bed, curling into a ball before wondering if that was the safest place for her to be. They'd changed the recommendations so many times since she was a kid that she was no longer sure.

The earthquake continued for a full minute. It felt like an eternity as the floor shook under her and things fell off the walls and shelves, the lights flickering on and off.

Finally, the house stopped shaking. Cheryl kept her eyes closed, holding her legs to her chest, panicked at the thought of another earthquake coming. She had no idea how to gauge the size of an earthquake, but that had been big.

Cheryl opened her eyes and screamed—a gecko was under the bed with her, only inches from her face.

"It's perfectly harmless," she whispered to herself, trying to calm herself down, but she still rolled away from it as quickly as she could, the jumped to her feet and stood next to the bed, hand on her heart.

Cheryl surveyed the damage. It didn't appear as if any

structural damage had happened, but so many of the cute knickknacks Susan had on shelves had fallen and broken.

After making sure her immediate surroundings were okay—that there was still power, the water still worked, and her phone still had service, Cheryl ventured outside to check on the neighbors.

The first thing she noticed was that a large tree had fallen onto the house just to her west—the one she shared a driveway with. Cheryl rushed over to see if anyone was home, praying if they were, that they were safe.

As she neared, she could hear a woman crying inside.

CHAPTER 8

*L*incoln sat in his car, gripping the steering wheel so hard his knuckles were white. That was an earthquake—it had to have been one. It confirmed that the earlier rumbling he'd felt was one too. He'd figured Cheryl was slamming doors or moving furniture or something like that.

Was she okay? This last one had felt strong. Not as strong as the one he'd experienced in Anchorage many years earlier, but definitely big.

Lincoln debated for a moment before deciding to continue with his quest to find a place to stay. Once he was settled in, he could go check on Cheryl. The earthquake hadn't been strong enough to cause serious damage, and the odds of her being injured were really, really slim. Odds of him finding a hotel with a vacancy were much slimmer, especially right after an earthquake. The hotels would probably fill up quickly.

Lincoln started forward again, keeping his eyes open for anyone who might need help, but the streets were empty. The vacation rental was in a little, remote village, and he hadn't seen hardly any other cars on his way in.

He didn't get very far before he had to stop. He scowled at the road. It had sustained damage from the earthquake.

Lincoln pulled to the side of the street and got out to inspect things, groaning in frustration. It looked like the ground had shifted downward, taking the road with it, creating a two-foot crevice in the asphalt. There was no way he'd be able to get out that way.

Already knowing what he'd find, he opened his maps application to see if there was another way out. The road he was on looped around, meeting up with a highway. Unfortunately, that road was the only one in and out, and he already knew the other half was torn up for construction. He'd had to go all the way around two days earlier just to get to the rental house.

"Crap," he muttered to himself.

Depending on how much damage there was to the rest of the island, he'd guess the construction wouldn't be a huge priority.

Lincoln rubbed the back of his neck. It looked like he'd be invading Cheryl's space again. Hopefully she'd understand.

With a sigh, he got back in his car and turned it around, heading to the vacation rental. As he drove, he started feeling nervous. If the road had that much damage to it, how would the rental have held up?

When he pulled into the drive and saw Cheryl trying to lift a tree that had fallen near the neighbor's house, relief washed over him. She appeared uninjured.

Lincoln got out of the car. "The road is collapsed. I can't go anywhere."

"Help me," Cheryl grunted.

Lincoln was about to tell her it would be impossible to lift the tree when he saw that most of it had landed *on* the house, not *next* to it. He stepped to Cheryl's side and heard a woman whimpering inside.

"Is she okay?" he asked Cheryl.

"Not sure."

Lincoln grabbed Cheryl's arm. "Come on, let's go find her. There's no way we'll be able to pull the tree up. They're a lot heavier than they look."

"We can't get inside—the tree crushed the front door."

"Is there another door?"

Cheryl shook her head. "I already looked."

"Then we'll go in through a window." He surveyed the windows. They were pretty high from the ground, especially with the house being built on stilts. These stilts were shorter than the vacation rental's, but they still lifted the window at least five feet from the ground. "I will, anyway."

Not waiting for her to answer, Lincoln stepped to the nearest one. It was locked.

He stepped back to where the tree had crushed part of the house. "Ma'am? Can you hear me?"

The whimpering stopped. "Yes, I can."

"Are you injured?"

"No, but my poor Kapua is stuck."

"Kapua?" Lincoln whispered to Cheryl.

"Her dog," Cheryl whispered back. "And her name is Nani."

He nodded, then spoke to the woman again. "We can't get inside the house unless we break a window. Are you okay with that?"

"Yes," Nani said. "Anything. I can't leave Kapua—I'm worried his crate will collapse."

"Are you the only one home right now, or is there anyone else?"

"It's just me and Kapua."

Lincoln looked around, searching for anything to break the window with. His eyes landed on a garden gnome, and he hefted it, pleased to find it was solid stone. He threw it at as hard as he could at the window he'd tried earlier, and the glass shattered.

Not hesitating, Lincoln pulled his shirt over his head, wrapped it around his hand several times, and broke the rest of the glass away. Then he folded the shirt in half twice, putting it over the jagged window edge before hoisting himself up and into the little bedroom on the other side.

Lincoln looked out at Cheryl and caught her staring at him. He hid a smile, but warmth spread through him at the expression of appreciation on her face. He was suddenly grateful he'd taken care of his body over the years. He wasn't sure why, but her appreciation made all the work feel worth it. "Do you want to come in?"

Cheryl eyed the window. "I'm not sure I can get over that thing. Don't worry about me—go help her."

"Okay. Do you want to check on other neighbors or wait here?"

She hesitated for a moment, then said, "I'd better stay in case you or Nani need me."

Good plan. "I'll be back."

Lincoln turned and gingerly stepped across the room, dodging things that had fallen.

He found Nani in what he assumed was a front room. The whole wall opposite him and the ceiling were now made up of the tree. Branches criss-crossed, and bits of light filtered in. The floor was covered in pieces of a bookshelf and books. The woman was on her knees, trying to reach through the branches for a dog crate where a little brown puppy shivered.

One glance at the damage in the room, and Lincoln knew Nani and her dog had been lucky—very lucky. The cage had protected Kapua from the bookcase when it collapsed, and somehow, all of the biggest branches had avoided landing on the dog.

Lincoln surveyed the situation. There was no way they'd be able to pull the dog and crate out the way things were now. He turned to Nani, putting a hand on her arm. It took a moment, but she finally focused her panicked eyes on him.

"Do you have any garden tools?" he asked. "Clippers? Trimmers? Anything like that?"

Nani chewed on her lip. "My husband might. I don't know. They'd be in the garage."

He eyed the crate. The dog was whimpering and crying, and taking its owner away would be a bad idea. "Give me a bit—I'll see what I can find."

She nodded, and Lincoln hurried back to the room he'd entered the house through. Cheryl was out there, wringing her hands, looking like she felt useless.

"I need your help. Can you come in?"

Cheryl surveyed the window. "Not without some serious assistance."

Lincoln turned around, spotting a chair by the bed. He cleared the glass off of it—a picture on the wall had fallen on it—and hefted it out the window. "Climb up. I'll help you over the rest of the way."

Cheryl positioned the chair under the window, having

to do some finagling to get it to balance correctly in the flower bed, then she hopped up. Lincoln leaned through the window and gave her a questioning look before touching her.

"Go ahead," she said, the expression on her face showing her hesitation. Without pause, he wrapped his hands around her waist and lifted. She was lighter than he'd expected. Not that she was big—she was anything but that—but he'd assumed she was roughly the same size as his last girlfriend. Not so. He pulled her against his chest as he backed into the room, and was surprised at the resulting emotions that exploded inside him. A burning desire to keep her in his arms, to protect her, to shelter her from any possible harm overwhelmed him.

He set her down but didn't release her immediately, pleased when she relaxed against him. But then Cheryl's eyes widened when she realized what she'd done. She stepped away as if burned. Lincoln's skin seared where she'd touched him, and a totally different desire flooded over him. Whoa—that was strong. Stronger than it'd ever been before. Had she felt it?

Cheryl looked down, clearing her throat. "What can I do?"

Oh, right. Nani and Kapua. "We need to search the garage for something to cut the branches."

"That's going to be hard. The tree landed on the garage, too. That's why I couldn't get in through it."

Lincoln and Cheryl walked to the garage. He groaned when they opened the door. The shelves near the big door had all been knocked over, their contents spewed everywhere. At least the damage was minimal so they wouldn't need to wade through branches to search the debris.

The two of them got to work immediately, but luckily, it didn't take nearly as long as Lincoln had feared to find trimmers they could use.

Lincoln led the way to the den and handed a pair of trimmers to Nani. "Let's clear as many branches as we can."

It took half an hour to cut a way to Kapua, and voices were sounding outside as Lincoln finagled the door on the crate open. Kapua bolted out, straight into Nani's arms, and the three of them got to their feet. Lincoln wiped sweat off of his brow. That had been a lot harder than he'd expected.

He and the two women walked back to where he and Cheryl had entered the house. Several concerned people stood outside, talking. Lincoln helped Nani and Kapua out, then turned to Cheryl.

"I can do it myself," she said. "It's not so bad on this side."

He tamped down on the disappointment that flared. She obviously didn't want him to touch her. Did that mean she hadn't felt the connection earlier? If not, it wasn't a connection then, just his hormones. Dang it.

The neighbors waiting outside thanked Lincoln and Cheryl, informed them that Nani's house was the only one really damaged, then promised to look after her and Kapua until help could arrive. They walked away, and Lincoln and Cheryl were left standing in the driveway.

"How bad is the road?" Cheryl asked.

Naturally, her first thought would be to get rid of him. Unfortunately for her, he was stuck. "Pretty bad, and I don't know how, since hardly anything seems to have been damaged here. I wouldn't be able to drive it even if I had a truck. I'm guessing there was a pocket of soft sand under it that caused it to drop."

Cheryl groaned. "Don't they squish down dirt before putting asphalt over it? Aren't things like that supposed to be prevented?" She groaned again. "How long do you think it'll take to repair?"

Do you have to make it so obvious you don't want me around?

Lincoln shrugged, playing it casual. "I don't know. I guess it would depend on how much damage is done across the whole island."

"There aren't any hotels in Captain Cook."

"I know."

"I guess you're staying at my vacation rental, then."

He chuckled. "*Your* vacation rental?"

She hesitated. "I mean, I *was* there first."

He shook his head. "I got in a full day before you. I heard you arrive last night."

"Ugh. Fine, I'll stay in *your* vacation rental."

Lincoln grinned at her, enjoying her snarky sense of humor. And it *was* humor—she'd had a slight smile on her lips as she said it.

He already knew he was attracted to her—their touch earlier had cemented that in for him—but before he could allow himself to think of the "what could be" between them, he shoved any thoughts of "them" away. This woman hated him. She obviously couldn't forgive, and he didn't want anything to do with someone like that. But also, no matter how likely it was that she'd get over her grudge, he'd been down that road with three other women, and there was no way he'd open up and get rejected again. Especially if his instincts were correct that he wasn't meant to get married.

Cheryl surprised Lincoln by offering to help carry his

stuff back into the house. He turned her down—he only had the one suitcase—but still, the offer made him realize it was in her nature to make people around her feel more comfortable, regardless of her personal feelings about them. Despite his vow to avoid her emotionally, he found himself wanting to learn how her past had shaped that trait.

Too bad, Lincoln. Too bad.

He wouldn't be doing that any time soon.

CHAPTER 9

Cheryl had just finished making herself breakfast when Lincoln knocked on the half wall that separated the stairs from the living area.

"Um . . . yes?" She wasn't sure how else to answer.

"Are you decent?"

Cheryl blinked. Why would he ask a question like that? Oh, he wanted to know if she was clothed. Did he really think she'd shed clothes as soon as they got back? Now that she knew he had to use her kitchen, there was no way she'd wander the upstairs in anything less than a full outfit.

"Of course."

"Are you okay if I cook another burrito?"

"*Another* one? Surely there's better food downstairs than that." Typical guy —wouldn't cook to save his life.

"There is . . . but I can't use the stove down there, and Cheryl . . ." He faded off, then cleared his throat. When he talked again, he sounded sheepish. "I don't want to be under your hair all the time. I can eat burritos—they'll get me back downstairs the fastest."

He was avoiding cooking to protect her from feeling uncomfortable? That touched her.

Lincoln finally stepped into her living room. His cheeks were pink and his hair tousled. Had he taken a quick nap? Or was he embarrassed and had been running a hand through his hair? The latter seemed more likely.

Cheryl jumped to her feet. "You are *not* having another burrito. I won't allow you to live off of frozen junk the whole time you're here. I'll throw something together for you."

Lincoln hesitated, then rushed into the kitchen, took her by the arm, and gently pushed her back into her chair. Cheryl's mind went blank at the contact, and her thoughts fled back to how it had felt earlier to be held against his bare chest.

Good. So, so good.

"You are *not* cooking for me. I'm completely capable of taking care of myself."

This, she had to see. Cheryl resumed eating her own food, and Lincoln banged around in the kitchen. She took her time eating, curious to see what he'd pull together. He surprised her by whipping up a hamburger gravy that he smothered over microwaved potatoes.

She raised an eyebrow, staring at him as he settled in to eat. She was both disappointed and grateful that he'd sat two seats away. Grateful because she didn't think she could stand to be so close to him again, but disappointed because she craved more physical contact. "I'm surprised. You really *do* know how to cook."

He gave her a half smile. "The stereotype about men not knowing their way around a kitchen is probably truer than it's not, but it isn't that way for me. I actually enjoy this."

Huh. Cool.

Cheryl left her thoughts at that. She wouldn't allow herself to imagine cooking with him or him cooking a romantic dinner for her. Or him bringing her breakfast in bed. Her cheeks burned at the thought.

Knock it off! You're making your life so much harder than it needs to be.

"How open are you to going for a walk with me?" Lincoln asked.

Cheryl froze. Like, a romantic walk? Holding hands? Strolling barefoot on the beach? Was he hoping for a friendship with her, now that they were stuck in the same place? Despite the thoughts she'd just lectured from her mind, she felt an inkling of hope that that was what he wanted.

Before she could answer, though, he rushed to say, "I know Nani's neighbors said damage hadn't been done elsewhere, but I want to check around and be sure. I don't know how well they know the area. There might be vacation rentals with people staying in them who are in trouble."

Despite her efforts not to allow emotions into the picture, disappointment crashed over her. That was so far from what she'd expected and even wanted. She ought to be ashamed of herself for assuming his only intention had been romance. She ground her teeth as she tried to process how quickly she'd jumped to conclusions. "That's a really good idea." She should have thought of that.

"They're probably right, but I want to be sure. Just in case."

"Yeah, just in case."

Lame answer. Save yourself before it's too late.

Cheryl gave some excuse about wanting to lie down

until he was ready to go, rinsed her dishes, then practically fled to her room. What she really needed was time away from him. Time to get her head set on straight. She did *not* want romance with him. And he didn't want it either— she'd learned that lesson in high school. So why did her thoughts keep going that way? If she didn't get in control of herself, she'd end up *really* doing something to embarrass herself. Like how things had gone back in high school. She'd always been awkward when she had a crush. Clumsy, ditzy, embarrassing herself over and over again.

Cheryl stared at herself in the bathroom mirror. That had been high school. And no, she wasn't super successful or doing what she'd dreamed of all growing up, but she was an adult now, and she did have a measure of confidence she'd lacked in high school.

Unfortunately, being around him brought back more than just memories.

She'd just have to find a way to prove to him *and* herself that she wasn't the awkward, shy, embarrassing high schooler anymore.

Cheryl only stayed in her room for a few minutes. She didn't want him to have to wait for her. Instead, she went out to the living room and sat on the couch where she could answer texts from everyone who'd heard about the earthquake. The fact that not many people had reached out told her it hadn't been very bad, and a quick glance at the headlines said the same thing. Not even the Hawaii papers gave it more than a casual mention.

Man, if *that* had felt like a big earthquake, Cheryl really hoped she'd never experience a truly big one.

LINCOLN WAS tireless as they drew out a map of the neighborhood, using an application on his phone as a reference, then walked the streets, knocking on doors, checking on people, and performing small acts of service. Cheryl couldn't help but be impressed. The man had boundless energy. Unlike her—she had *bound* energy. She was exhausted, and she felt that to her bones, after only a few houses. But what did she expect? She had a desk job, and he walked an entire rehab center all day long.

Still, despite the tiredness that filled her body, Cheryl found herself having fun. Lincoln's enthusiasm was contagious, and not an ounce of his concern was fabricated. He truly did enjoy serving others. He'd been that way in high school, but not enough for her to have remembered until now. He'd obviously spent a great deal of time in the service of other people, and had developed that trait into something truly attractive.

They dug out belongings, cleaned up broken things, and found other pets—including a gecko. Why would anyone who had geckos running around them all day every day keep one as a pet? Mind boggled.

They even helped someone round up a bunch of chickens. Where Cheryl found the gecko humorous, Lincoln really got a kick out of the chickens—wild ones were literally everywhere on the island, but the woman wanted *her* specific chickens. And every wrong chicken Cheryl and Lincoln brought back, the woman somehow knew it wasn't hers.

When they'd rounded all of them up, Cheryl couldn't tell a difference between the wild ones and the chickens the woman claimed. She supposed it might have been like her kids, though—to someone on the outside, they looked a lot like other teenagers their age, but Cheryl knew exactly who they were.

Either way, when she and Lincoln left, the woman was beaming with happiness. Despite her crankiness, Cheryl's heart warmed. She really needed to get out of her little family more often.

She was ready to hit the sack only an hour after they left the vacation rental. Despite her exasperation with Lincoln's energy, though, she felt herself softening toward him when the odd requests and different challenges didn't faze him.

Serving people was second nature to him. Cheryl really could learn a thing or two about that from him—most days, she had to remind herself that other people existed. Work and the kids were so all-consuming it was hard to remember that she wasn't the only one who stressed and struggled.

Lincoln obviously wasn't new to that idea. In fact, he seemed to thrive off of what they were doing.

So, despite her aching feet and exhausted legs, Cheryl continued following him for what seemed like hours, getting to know people, finding those who needed help, and being of service as much as they could.

Their conversation wasn't deep—not once did it stray from the task at hand. A couple of times, Cheryl wondered if Lincoln was keeping it superficial on purpose. Maybe he was just that focused on what they were doing, but they had plenty of opportunities to extend the conversation beyond the current tasks at hand. And she had so many questions for him.

Like, what had he been up to since high school? Why was he single? Had he ever been married? What was his family doing? Did he have kids? Did he know *she* had kids and had been married? How would he react to her story and situation?

And most importantly, what had happened the night he stood her up? Why hadn't he reached out to her? If nothing had come up and he simply just didn't want to go out with her in the first place—which she expected was the case—why hadn't he just told her no when she'd asked him out?

Ugh. So many questions. And absolutely no courage to bring any of them up. Cheryl found herself just as tongue-tied and hesitant around him as she'd been in high school, and that really frustrated her. How long would it take for her to be herself again? Had she really bottled up her entire high school experience and not allowed herself to get over it and move on?

She wasn't surprised by the sheer number of questions that rolled around in her brain the whole time she and Lincoln scoured the neighborhood. What did surprise her, though, was learning that they hadn't been at it for several hours like she'd thought. Two hours. Only *two hours* had passed since they'd started their quest to help neighbors.

If that wasn't evidence that Cheryl was out of shape, she didn't know what was.

"Ready for food?" Lincoln asked.

Cheryl glanced at him, then beyond, surprised to see that they were only a couple hundred feet from the vacation rental. She hadn't even noticed they'd made their way back. The little alleys and roads had all started blending together.

"Definitely. I'm starving."

"How are you holding up?" Lincoln paused, turning to Cheryl. "It just occurred to me that you're probably not used to this."

She hesitated. Tell him the truth or act casual? That was a no-brainer. "I'm exhausted. My job isn't nearly this physically demanding."

Lincoln reached out and briefly touched her arm. "I'm really sorry. I should have been more considerate."

Cheryl told him it was okay, but her thoughts went far from his apology and landed on the contact he'd made with her. Despite the fact that it had been brief, her skin still tingled where he'd touched her, and she didn't—*couldn't*—ignore the fact that she wanted more of it. Furthermore, she was too tired to lecture it out of herself.

"What do you do for work, anyway?" he asked as they started walking again.

"I'm surprised my mom hasn't already told you," Cheryl said. "I'm a receptionist at Alpine Hospital. I work in the cardiology department."

"Oh, that's right. She told me her daughter worked there, but that was before I'd made the connection that it was you."

Under normal circumstances, Cheryl was supposed to then ask him what he did for work, but she already knew, and despite all of her earlier questions, she had no idea what to say or ask next. Her earlier questions were too deep. Now that they were finally having a conversation that didn't involve chickens and geckos, she didn't want to ruin it.

As it turned out, she didn't need to come up with anything because there were people sitting on the porch when they arrived.

Cheryl paused for a moment, studying the woman, then her eyes widened with excitement. "Susan?"

The woman looked up. "Cheryl!"

Cheryl rushed forward and gave the woman a hug.

"What are you doing here? Mom said you guys live in Hilo and that I wouldn't see you at all."

Susan's husband, Tom, shook her hand.

"Tom is a disaster psychologist. The state wants him here, where most of the damage happened." Susan chewed on her lip, obviously not sure how to say what was on her mind. Cheryl suspected she knew what was coming, though.

"You need your space back, don't you?" Dismay flooded through Cheryl. Where would she stay? If the road was down, she couldn't exactly get out and find a hotel.

"Yes, we do. I'm so very sorry about that, but there literally isn't anywhere else we can go."

Cheryl nodded, trying to tamp down her disappointment. Maybe she could stay with the chicken lady.

Susan obviously noticed Cheryl's disappointment because she rushed to say, "We have three bedrooms in the basement. I'm sure Lincoln wouldn't mind squeezing over and making room for you down there."

Cheryl's mind went blank. She had absolutely no answer for that, and despite all the emotions she'd experienced that day, not even her heart had anything in it. Then the shock hit her. *Stay with Lincoln?*

Lincoln came to her rescue. "Definitely. I don't need a lot of room—Cheryl can take what she needs."

Susan didn't seem convinced, probably because Cheryl had clammed up. She studied Cheryl again before turning to Lincoln and saying, "Thank you so much. The kitchen down there is pretty much done—it just needs mudding, taping, and painting, plus putting the sink back in, but everything works. And Tom can do the sink now, if you'd be able to help him."

"Of course," Lincoln said. "I've done it before."

"Great."

The two men left to do that, and Susan put a hand on Cheryl's arm. "I'm sorry, I really am. When duty calls, Tom has to answer."

Cheryl finally found her voice. "Please don't apologize —I completely understand." She just didn't know how she was going to stay in the same apartment as Lincoln. She'd already been struggling with the idea of being in the same house, for crying out loud.

"How much damage was done from the earthquake?" she asked.

"Honestly, not much—the epicenter was several miles from here, out in the ocean. A couple of the highways were damaged. Lamentable, but all of them needed to be built stronger anyway. Despite there not being a lot of damage, it still has disrupted lives—especially with not being able to leave by car until the roads are fixed."

"How'd you guys get here?"

"By boat. We have two houses—this one, and the one in Hilo. We keep enough here where if we had to stay for a couple of weeks, we'd be comfortable."

Why the boat thing hadn't occurred to Cheryl, she wasn't sure. It seemed obvious, now, though. Hawaii was surrounded by water.

Susan linked arms with Cheryl. "Let's go see what the boys are up to, shall we? We might be able to help them in some way. Plus, I'm starving." She glanced over at Cheryl as they walked up the stairs to the porch. "We'd love to have you up for dinner, but after that, you'll be on your own—we won't see you much."

Cheryl almost rushed to ask them to stick around, but she held her tongue. The people in the area needed Tom's skills, and Susan obviously would want to help him as much as possible. Cheryl sighed to herself as the two women entered the basement apartment. Her confusion and discomfort where Lincoln was concerned couldn't be helped by the home owners.

Cheryl took in the large room they'd just entered. Huge windows lined an entire wall, there were two comfy couches, and the kitchen was good sized. Plenty of space. But would it be enough for her not to feel like she was constantly running into Lincoln? She didn't think so.

The men were hooking up the plumbing, completely absorbed in their task, and Susan turned to Cheryl. "I'll get dinner started. Why don't you grab your things and move them down?"

Cheryl nodded, and Susan left. Cheryl hesitated, though. Which room was supposed to be hers? She could ask, but she didn't want to distract Lincoln from what he was doing. Though . . . she knew deep down that what she really didn't want was to draw attention to herself.

She'd put her things on one of the couches until Lincoln could point her in the right direction. No way was she going to explore on her own and end up in his bedroom.

Decision made, Cheryl headed upstairs to her former room, lost in her thoughts. In one day, she'd gone from having a vacation rental all to herself to sharing an apartment with a man she hated.

How was she going to survive this?

And no, she found she didn't hate him anymore. After spending several hours with him, watching him serve, help, and bless the lives of those affected by the earthquake, she *couldn't* hate him. She couldn't even dislike him anymore—more than once, she'd even felt an inkling of her years' earlier crush. But that didn't mean she wasn't uncomfortable with the new arrangements.

Especially if her crush returned in full bloom. Ugh. How would she handle that? She put her face in her hands and leaned against the four-poster bed. This vacation was causing her more stress than it was relieving.

Cheryl quickly packed her things, zipped her suitcase, then grabbed her Dr Pepper from the upstairs fridge and headed downstairs. She put the suitcase on one of the couches and the Dr Pepper in the fridge. At that point, the men were just finishing with caulking around the sink and cleaning up their work station. Cheryl stood near her suitcase, waiting for them, not sure what to do with herself now.

Tom shook Lincoln's hand. "Thanks for your help. I'd say I'd knock it off your rent, but Susan told me how much you're paying to stay, and I don't think you'd even notice."

Lincoln chuckled. "No, this has been a very affordable trip. Thank you both so much—I really appreciate it."

"Yes, well, I'm sorry we've crashed the party. We'll be out of your hair most of the time, though. I expect to be gone from sunup to sundown every day."

"Good to know."

Tom headed upstairs to help Susan with dinner, and Lincoln turned to Cheryl who was standing awkwardly in the living room.

They surveyed each other for a moment. Cheryl studied Lincoln's face, noting the stress lines around his eyes. She couldn't tell if he was stressed because she'd be in his territory or because he was worried for her.

"I'm sorry," she said.

He blinked, surprised. "You don't have anything to be sorry for."

"Yes, I do. I was rude to you earlier, after the earthquake. I know that was this morning, but I still feel awful for it. It doesn't matter what grudge I hold against you or how you wronged me twenty years ago—" Even *she* recognized the ridiculousness of her situation "—none of this is your fault."

Lincoln took a step toward her, his expression earnest. "I feel bad for what happened too. There's no way I would have come if I'd known your mom was arranging things to be like this."

Cheryl put her hand in her face and groaned. "Mom. And yes, she admitted to everything."

Lincoln chuckled. "Sounds about right for Helen."

Cheryl didn't look up, but she nodded. It definitely did.

"So, truce?" Lincoln asked.

She looked up. "Yes. Truce."

Lincoln seemed to relax, the stress lines leaving his face, and Cheryl had to admit to feeling better herself. But still, there was one major thing that hadn't yet been resolved.

"Where am I staying?" she asked.

"You can have the big room."

"Was that where you've been sleeping?"

Lincoln nodded. "But I'm fine moving."

Cheryl shook her head. "No. I'll take one of the other rooms. I've already packed my things up. It'll be easier for me to go into an empty room than it would be for you to move."

Besides, she really *was* on his turf. It was best not to

ruffle feathers and make her presence known more than it already was.

Lincoln led the way down the hall, opening the first door to the left, revealing a peach-colored bedroom. The bed was a twin, and the room had a lot of family things in it like stuffed animals, pictures, and books, but it was clean and well organized. Definitely better than hunting for a hotel that didn't exist.

Cheryl dumped her suitcase on the floor by the bed, then turned and thanked Lincoln.

"Now what?" he asked.

Cheryl's tummy did a little flip. He expected them to spend more time together? It made her insides happy to think he actually wanted that. He couldn't possibly be repulsed by the idea—not given his guarded, though eager expression. But maybe she was reading too much into his question. Maybe he wasn't asking if they should do something together.

Either way, Cheryl had had enough socializing for the day. She needed as much quiet time now as she could get. "I'd like to clean up and rest, if that's all right. Take a shower."

Lincoln immediately nodded. "Oh, yeah, great idea. I'd like a shower as well."

Heat flooded Cheryl's cheeks. "But not together."

Lincoln's face turned crimson. "That's what it sounded like I said, but that's *definitely* not what I meant. I mean, not *definitely*—I'm sure a shower with you would be anything but bad—but it wouldn't be appropriate and things are already going to be awkward with us staying in the same apartment." He slammed his mouth shut as if realizing he'd been rambling. The redness seeped into his neck. He cleared his throat. "No, not together."

A giggle popped out of Cheryl's mouth. She was glad she wasn't the only one who said embarrassing things.

Lincoln rushed onward. "I'll shower first, if you're okay with that. That way, you won't feel like I'm waiting for you."

Cheryl nodded, grateful. "That would be wonderful. Thank you."

This man really was a good guy. He'd been putting other people first all day. And as much as she wanted to put *him* first for a change, she knew he was right—there was no way she'd relax if she knew he was waiting, and she desperately needed the quiet and peace a shower would bring.

She vowed to start putting him first just as soon as she could. But she'd take this last act of service gratefully.

Her appreciation had him smiling, and he stepped out of the doorway, walking down the hall and entering a room at the end.

Cheryl shut her door, then slumped into a chair by the desk, completely and totally drained.

At this rate, she'd need a vacation after her vacation.

CHAPTER 10

*L*incoln knew he was right about one thing—Cheryl would have thought about him the whole time she was showering if she'd gone first. There was no way she wouldn't have. He already knew by then that she didn't like to impose on other people or get attention, and knowing he waited would have prevented her from relaxing.

"Go fast, go fast, go fast," he muttered to keep himself on task and not dawdle. He could see the exhaustion written all over her face earlier and didn't want to deprive her of even just one second. Especially since she was no longer treating him like Enemy Number One. He wanted to stay on her good side.

Lincoln was impressed by how stalwart and strong Cheryl had been during their excursions all over the area. He still felt bad for setting such a strong and rapid pace—he should have remembered earlier that not everyone was used to it—but the woman had kept up like a champ. She'd obviously been puzzled, amused, and even a little irritated with the chicken situation, but she hadn't complained once.

The woman didn't have a bad bone in her body. It made him feel even worse for not having explained what happened that night so long ago. But he couldn't just blurt it out—he needed to wait until he could explain it so she'd recognize the gravity of the situation, so he could help her see just how stressful that evening had been for him. But when would that opportunity come up? Would he have to artificially create it? Or would something naturally happen, where talking about things that still obviously hurt her would be possible?

He wasn't sure. But he knew one thing—he wasn't leaving this island until he had a chance to try to make things right with her again.

Lincoln hopped out of the shower and dried off, then dressed in clean clothes, combed his hair so it wouldn't dry ridiculously, and exited the bathroom. He put his shoes on, then knocked on Cheryl's door as he walked past.

She opened up immediately, making him jump. "Shower's all yours," he said.

"That was really fast. Is the shower easy to use?"

"It's pretty normal. The bathroom is that door." He pointed at the correct one. "I'm heading upstairs to help with dinner. Feel free to take your time—I'll let them know it might be a bit."

Cheryl practically slumped against the door jamb. "Thank you. So much. I really appreciate it."

"It's the least I could do after crashing your vacation rental."

She gave him a small smile. "I thought it was *yours*."

He shrugged. "*You* know the owners. It's obvious you had the prior claim."

She studied his face, and he wished he could ask her what was on her mind. He also wished he could take her into his arms again, but by the way she held herself, that wouldn't be welcome. Cheryl still had a lot of walls around her, and that was totally fine. Lincoln did too. He hoped she'd drop a few of them while they were in Hawaii, though.

Dinner was enjoyable. It was interesting to see Cheryl open up around people she cared for and trusted. They got her laughing many times, and Lincoln found himself wanting to be funny, to get her to laugh and relax around him too.

Once they'd finished eating and Susan was serving up some chocolate pie she'd pulled out of the freezer, Tom steepled his fingers and said, "Lincoln, you mentioned earlier that the two of you were out meeting with people —making sure they were okay after the earthquake. Why don't you tell us what you encountered so we have a better idea of what to expect?"

Lincoln glanced at Cheryl, motioning for her to go ahead. He was interested in hearing what her take was on the people.

"Pretty much everyone was okay. We didn't come across anyone who'd been injured. A few things in everyone's houses had been damaged, but your neighbor had the most damage."

"Poor Nani," Susan muttered, a concerned expression on her face. "Where is she now? She wasn't there when we checked."

"She and Kapua went to stay with some neighbors," Cheryl said.

"We aren't sure which ones," Lincoln said, "but they seemed to know each other pretty well."

Cheryl then told Susan and Tom about the chicken experience. Susan knew immediately who she was referring to.

She shook her head slowly, chuckling. "Oh, Mahina. You and your chickens." She shook her head again. "That woman knows practically every chicken on this part of the island. Hers respond to her and usually come when she calls. She works hard to develop relationships with them from when they're little chicks. They let her hold them. They trust her as much as Kapua trusts Nani."

Lincoln nodded. "Makes sense, now, why she'd want them back and not one of the hundreds of random, wild ones we came across."

Cheryl half laughed, and Lincoln imagined she still struggled with the idea.

"Don't chickens only live a few years?" Cheryl asked. "That's a lot of work to have to repeat over and over again."

Susan nodded. "Hence why she wants *her* particular chickens."

"Well, I'm glad to know now why she was so particular," Cheryl said. "I'm also glad I got to meet all of the other chickens on the island, too."

The others at the table chuckled. Lincoln couldn't keep his eyes off of Cheryl. This side of her was enchanting.

"Anything else we should know?" Tom asked.

Cheryl meet Lincoln's gaze and shrugged.

"I'm not sure," Lincoln said, "but please let everyone know I'm a physical therapist, and if there are any injuries, I'd be more than happy to take a look at them. As long as they're not serious, I could help get them on the path to healing again."

"Thank you for offering—I'm sure some will take you up on that."

Lincoln nodded. "And Cheryl works in a cardiology department. She could probably—"

"Set up appointments in Utah," Cheryl said. "You know, if they want to make the trip there. I can also answer any questions they might have about their bills. But only the ones at Alpine Hospital."

Everyone laughed again, then Susan said, "What happened to your idea to get your beauty license?"

Cheryl flushed, and her eyes flitted to Lincoln's, then away. "It was only one of many ideas I had for what to do with my life."

"Are things going okay, then?" Susan asked.

From the expression on Cheryl's face, Lincoln could tell they weren't, but also from that expression, that she didn't want to discuss them.

"Her mom is always talking about how proud she is of Cheryl," Lincoln said, wanting to direct attention away from her. "How she has her entire office wrapped around her little finger—how the doctors and medical assistants are willing to do pretty much anything and everything for her."

Cheryl's mouth popped open. "That's not true. Did my mom really tell you that?"

Lincoln nodded. "I'm inclined to believe her stories," he said to Cheryl. "Helen isn't prone to exaggerating—she's been right about everything else she's said about you so far."

Cheryl's face went white. "What else has she said?"

Nothing too personal, and Lincoln rushed to reassure her. "Nothing embarrassing. She basically brags that you're a hard worker and rarely complain. That you're the most patient mom in the world and that your kids idolize you."

Cheryl shook her head. "I don't know—those two give me a lot of grief."

"They're teenagers," Susan said. "Their *job* is to push buttons. It's how they operate."

"Tell me about it," Tom said. "I'm so glad Susan and I are done raising kids—that's not something I want to ever do again." He paused. "It *was* worth the grandkids, though."

Susan grinned. "Grandkids make everything better."

"Hopefully, I'm a long way away from that," Cheryl said. "Xander is only sixteen, and Jade is fourteen."

Xander and Jade. Lincoln liked the names. He couldn't help but wonder where their dad was—that was one of many details Helen hadn't shared with him. The only thing she'd said was it hadn't worked out between them.

"Yeah, well, I'm even farther away from grandparenthood," Lincoln said. "I don't even have kids."

"Why not?" Tom asked.

It was Lincoln's turn to need to be rescued, but instead, the two women looked at him with curious expressions.

"Marriage just hasn't ever worked out. Trust me, I tried." He'd had those three opportunities, but each woman had turned him down.

"I'm sorry to hear that," Susan said. "You seem like an excellent man. You're on vacation, and yet, you've spent most of it helping other people. The woman who snags you will be one lucky person."

Instead of responding to Susan right away, Lincoln's gaze found its way to Cheryl. That was the last place he should have looked, but it was like his eyes weren't under his control, and he struggled to get them to look anywhere else. Her expression was concerned, confused, and curious. Three C words that would open a whole can of worms if she asked what she wanted to know.

He didn't dwell on what Susan had said. His knowledge that he wasn't meant to get married had sunk deep inside him, and he'd learned long ago not to hold onto the hope offered by people on the outside looking in.

He wasn't going there right then. Not over dinner, and definitely not surrounded by strangers. Still, a response was merited, and he didn't want to offend his hosts.

"Let's just hope she remembers that, years into the marriage when things aren't as romantic and exciting." Lincoln groaned inwardly. He should have just kept his mouth shut. What a clichéd thing to say.

"Yes, that's what we'll hope for," Susan said. Then, obviously sensing a change in topic was appropriate, said, "Well, thanks again for your help today, you two. We have a lot ahead of us tomorrow, so Tom and I will be heading to bed early."

"I'll help clean up," Cheryl said.

Lincoln got to his feet. "No, I'll do it." No way was he letting Cheryl stand on her feet after making her walk around all day.

Susan shook her head. "Don't worry, either of you. I haven't been in this home for months. It'll be good to figure out where our renters and cleaners have been putting things—take stock of what's missing and what needs to be fixed or replaced. Why don't you two go relax?"

The way she said it made Lincoln wonder if she thought they were a couple. Or maybe he was reading into it too much. Probably. He hated it when he overthought things.

Knowing Cheryl would probably want alone time again—she *was* on vacation by herself, after all—Lincoln settled onto the couch downstairs with his latest mystery novel.

Cheryl stood in the kitchen for a moment before making a decision on what she wanted to do. He knew she wasn't waiting for him to say something to her—her pause seemed to be internal. It occurred to him that she wasn't used to not having someone around her to serve. She'd been a mom for so long, maybe, that she wasn't sure how to function just as herself.

Even when Cheryl disappeared into her bedroom, Lincoln was still aware of her presence. His entire body seemed to be on hyper alert, every cell calling at him to put himself in close proximity to the woman again.

But no, he'd ignore those urges. His book was good, Cheryl had had a lot happen to her that day, and she probably needed some time to figure things out on her own. He forced himself to concentrate on the story in his hand.

He'd just started getting very involved when she quietly walked through the room and headed outside, probably going to the beach.

The beach was an excellent place to go when one needed to be alone.

He'd have to go there later himself.

Susan and Tom were already gone the next morning.

Lincoln wasn't surprised by that—they'd pretty much made it known they wouldn't be there a lot the night before. Still, the house already felt big and empty without them.

Lincoln found a note on the downstairs fridge from Susan.

There isn't a lot of food in the basement. Go ahead and eat what you find upstairs—we have plenty of storage to draw from for times like these.

Having been given permission to rummage, Lincoln went upstairs. As he dug around the Tupperware and heavily sealed packages, his thoughts strayed to Cheryl. He realized he hadn't known her all that well in high school. She was funny, intelligent, and spunky.

She was also charitable and selfless. He still couldn't believe she'd been okay with taking the smaller room. His own tall frame wouldn't fit on that bed. And yes, she was fairly petite, but surely she was used to sleeping on something a little bigger.

The woman obviously didn't recognize her own virtues, judging by how she'd reacted to what her mom had told him. Helen had said a lot of good things about her daughter before their initial encounter in his facility. He now recognized why—she wanted to strike interest in him before he had a chance to meet her, or rather, re-meet her. Had she known who he was and how he was connected to Cheryl? He wasn't sure. She'd definitely succeeded in getting him interested in her daughter. Not from their conversations about her—those had been casual and about someone he thought he wouldn't ever meet—but from getting him stuck in the same place as Cheryl. He was seeing sides to her he knew he wouldn't ever have had the chance to see back home, even if they'd dated. At least, he wouldn't have seen those sides for a long time.

Lincoln carried the ingredients downstairs, determined to make a big breakfast for his "roommate." She deserved it after yesterday.

He was nearly finished cooking when Cheryl finally emerged from her room. She wore jeans and a T that emphasized made her perfect curves. He had to look away —his eyes wanted to explore her, to soak in her beautiful figure, but he didn't want to burn the eggs or make her uncomfortable. It was hard not to look back again, though.

Cheryl paused at the entrance to the room, and he felt her gaze on him. He finally dared to glance her way again. He was surprised to see tears in her eyes.

She gestured to the table, already set for two, and the food he'd laid out. "I haven't had an actual breakfast in years."

Really? Wow. "I hope this one doesn't disappoint you."

"I'm sure it won't. It smells delicious."

Lincoln put the eggs on the table, then took a seat, inviting her to sit as well.

"Too busy to eat breakfast, maybe?" he asked.

She nodded, buttering her pancake on both sides. "Work, the kids, their homework, food, and cleaning the house definitely keep me on my toes."

"Tell me about your kids. They're sixteen and fourteen?"

"Yes. Xander is the older of the two, and Jade is the younger one."

He'd remembered Jade's name, but couldn't recall Xander's. "They're good kids, then?"

"Pretty much. Xander is a bit rebellious at times, but

he's calmed down a great deal since my brother, Jack, came back."

"Where was Jack?"

"He's a former senator. He only served one term, then decided to move home so he could help with my mom when she had her fall and surgery."

Good for him. Lincoln already knew that Helen was a widow—her husband had passed away a few years earlier. She needed Jack there to help her out.

"You haven't met him yet?" Cheryl asked.

Lincoln shook his head. "Looking back, I think your mom purposefully only invited you over when I was around. It took her a few tries to get us in the same room, though."

Cheryl groaned, dropping her head in embarrassment. "Mom, seriously?"

Lincoln laughed. "It's not such a big deal—I'm used to patients doing that. Most of them know someone single, and a lot of them try to set me up."

"And that doesn't bother you?"

He shook his head. "It doesn't ever lead anywhere. Most of the time, we don't click when we meet, and it's obvious one or the other of us isn't attracted."

Cheryl knitted her eyebrows together. "I don't care what anyone says—attraction is very important, regardless of age."

The way she said it—sort of sadly—told him she didn't think she was attractive. How was that possible? The woman was pretty amazing. Could he say anything that would help her see her beauty and that wouldn't creep her out or be coming on too strong? He wasn't sure, but he had to try.

"Your ex-husband was an idiot to let you go."

She half shrugged. "Who says *I* didn't let *him* go?"

"That's exactly what I'm saying. He was a total idiot for not recognizing the blessings he'd been given. Cheryl, I didn't know you very well in high school, but what I've seen the last two days is nothing short of perfection."

Cheryl's eyes widened, in a deer-in-headlights way.

Definitely too strong.

"What I'm trying to say," he rushed to continue, "is I think you're a great person. Don't sell yourself short or try to convince yourself that your husband came out on top somehow. Because he didn't."

And now he was starting to sound like a best friend or a pal or something like that. But was that bad? What *did* he want, anyway? He wasn't sure. Okay, physically, he was positive he wanted nothing more than to pull her into his arms and take her to his bedroom. But what did he want emotionally? Mentally?

He hoped he'd figure it out. Something—a fear of missing out, maybe—told him he didn't want to screw things up. But *was* he wanting to give a relationship a try?

Get real, dude. You still haven't come clean with her on anything yet. She probably won't want you when she finds out you got back with your ex instead of going out with her.

That wasn't exactly true. The *accident* had kept him from the date. The *accident* had derailed his entire life. But he *had* gotten back with his ex, and Cheryl had despised him for years.

He needed to have the conversation with her, and soon. She wouldn't open up to him until he did, and for reasons he didn't quite understand, it was important to him that she *did* open up. He wanted to understand what made her tick, what got her out of bed every morning, what made her happy and what made her cry.

Just thinking those thoughts was enough to make him panic, to make his heart double in speed, his palms sweat. *Too soon, Lincoln. Too soon. Get back to safer topics.*

"Do you want to see if we can find more people today who need help? I promise we'll take a slower pace this time."

"Even though Susan and Tom are here now?"

"Why not?" It would give them something to do— something that would make them both feel useful. When he said as much to her, she nodded, obviously understanding how he felt.

"Let's do it."

They cleaned up breakfast, saving the leftovers, and headed out to the one area they still hadn't reached. The one with nice houses along the ocean. Neither of them had ever voiced it before, but they'd left those places to the very last. Lincoln wasn't sure why. It wasn't like the uber rich couldn't have bad things happen to them too—far from it. Some of his patients were very wealthy, and yet, they'd ended up in his rehab center just like the rest. But still, he'd hesitated.

The two of them walked with purpose toward those houses. There was a little cluster of them on the beach, not far from each other.

No one answered the first door they knocked, and Lincoln wasn't surprised. The place practically screamed "Empty vacation rental." So they went on to the next house. The people who answered were polite and didn't need anything.

"Do you know anything about your neighbors?" Cheryl asked. "Have you heard from any of them since the earthquake?"

The man shook his head. "No, sorry. We're not from here."

Lincoln thanked him, and he and Cheryl walked to the next house.

Cheryl raised her hand to knock, then hesitated, turning her big green eyes toward Lincoln. "Can you hear that?" she asked.

He paused, then noticed what had caught her attention. Faint crying, and a lot of it. "Is it coming from inside?"

"Yes." She knocked on the door, then rang the doorbell.

The crying didn't stop, and no one came.

Cheryl tried the knob, and before Lincoln could tell her not to, she'd opened the door and stepped inside.

"Cheryl!" he hissed, both impressed with her brazenness and appalled that she'd enter uninvited. "Isn't that called breaking and entering?"

She didn't respond, instead rushing toward the sounds of the crying.

The house was huge, and it took several seconds to get through the front entry and to the back where the cries were coming from.

The moment they'd entered a large combined kitchen and living room, though, Lincoln knew Cheryl had been right to barge in. An older woman was lying on the floor, gripping her chest, her face pale, gasping for air. A teenage girl was kneeling next to her, sobbing.

Cheryl rushed to the girl's side, dropping beside her. "What's going on?" she asked, loudly enough to be heard over the girl's crying.

"She just fell over! I think she's having a heart attack!"

Cheryl took the woman's hand, checking the pulse in

her wrist, and glanced up at Lincoln. "Get a cold, wet rag."

Lincoln jumped to do so, returning as Cheryl finished calculating the woman's heartbeat. She dialed a number on her phone, and Lincoln was surprised to see it wasn't 911.

"Dr. Tuttle, hi. Yes, good. I have a woman here who might be having a heart attack. Because of the earthquake, we're pretty much stuck without emergency services. Tell me what to do."

Oh, that's right. An ambulance wouldn't be able to get there. Calling the office back home was a really good idea.

Cheryl put the phone on speakerphone, setting it on the tile beside her.

"What is her heart rate?" a man's voice asked.

"Around hundred and thirty beats per minute, but it was hard to count fast enough to keep up."

"That's pretty high. What happened leading up to the incident?"

Cheryl looked at the teenager, and the girl wrung her hands. "She was talking about the earthquake," the girl said. "Freaking out, really. And she said it was going to cause so many problems, especially for my brother who's been trying to get home."

Dr. Tuttle seemed to want to keep the girl talking because he said, "Tell me about your brother."

"He's in the military. Stationed in Oahu. He was supposed to come home today."

While the teenager continued talking to Dr. Tuttle about her brother, Cheryl turned to Lincoln. "Would you get a pillow and blanket? We need to get her as comfortable as possible."

Lincoln nodded, then went off in search of the items.

He found both in one of the massive bedrooms down a hall, then returned to Cheryl. The two of them covered the woman and lifted her head onto the pillow, then Lincoln turned his attention back to the conversation.

"What's your grandma's name?" Dr. Tuttle was asking.

"Ardith."

"Ardith? Can you hear me?"

The woman groaned in response, then rasped, "Yes."

"Tell me about the pain. What does it feel like?"

"Sharp stabbing. In my heart."

"How else are you feeling?"

"Nauseated . . . Weak . . . Lightheaded . . ." The woman reached up to brush hair off her face, her hand trembling. "Can't catch breath . . ."

Dr. Tuttle was silent for a moment. "How are your hands and arms doing?"

"Arms . . . fine. Hands tingling."

"She's trembling a lot," Cheryl said.

"Good to know." Dr. Tuttle was silent for a moment. "Chloe, could you tell me again what your grandmother was doing when the attack happened?"

"She'd just gotten off the phone with my brother," Chloe said.

"Okay, thank you. Cheryl, would you get her comfortable? Give her a pillow and blanket."

"Will do." Cheryl gave Lincoln a smile of gratitude and mouthed the word "thanks," though he wasn't sure why—it had been her idea in the first place. "Anything else?"

"Can you stay with her for an hour or two?"

Lincoln and Cheryl met eyes again. "That's not a problem," Cheryl said.

"Good. I suspect she's having a panic attack. If the pain lets off, that's what it is. If it doesn't, well, let's hope the roads open up soon."

Chloe glanced up. "She's had panic attacks before, but nothing like this."

"Bad panic attacks are very, very similar to heart attacks," Dr. Tuttle said. "One of the major differences is in how the pain presents—panic typically causes a stabbing pain. Heart attacks cause a burning and sometimes squeezing pain. And they usually happen after activity, though not always. Panic attacks are triggered by extremely stressful events—like an earthquake—or the buildup of multiple stressful things. Your brother not being able to come back, plus the earthquake, plus the roads being closed—these are all things that could lead to severe panic."

"And the fact that she's had them before, right?" Cheryl said.

"Exactly. Pain from panic usually dissipates, whereas heart attack pain typically sticks around."

"Already fading," Ardith said.

"Wonderful. Let's see if it goes all the way away. Cheryl, keep me updated on her condition. You have my number."

"When can we move her?"

"When she's feeling up to it, but only move her once—don't get carried away. No walks all the way to the beach."

Ardith waved at the window. "It's in my backyard . . . Not far away."

Dr. Tuttle chuckled. "Lucky."

Cheryl ended the call, then turned her attention to the older woman. "Would you like us to move you to the couch?"

"Yes. Chloe can turn on . . . a movie."

"Pick something relaxing," Cheryl said to the girl before looking at Lincoln. "You up to helping me again?"

Of course he was. Moving people around was what he did all day, every day.

The two of them got her to her feet, then navigated her around the couch and into a recliner. After Cheryl tucked the blanket around Ardith, she plopped onto the couch, and Lincoln sat next to her. He fidgeted with his phone for a moment, feeling restless after all the earlier energy of the visit.

"Want to play a game while you're here?" Chloe asked, obviously sensing that their guests might be uncomfortable.

"Sure," Lincoln said, leaning forward. "What did you have in mind?"

The girl picked out a version of *Uno* Lincoln hadn't played before, and he, Cheryl, and Chloe sat on the floor to play while Ardith watched her movie. Lincoln kept an eye on her, and to his relief, she appeared to be improving. Her cheeks were no longer white, her pupils weren't dilated anymore, and the trembling had gone away. It seemed Dr. Tuttle was correct in his unofficial diagnosis.

When the game was finished, Ardith promised to go see a doctor as soon as the roads opened up, and Lincoln helped Cheryl to her feet—loving the feel of her hand in his, wishing he could prolong the contact. They left the house after Chloe had thanked them over and over again.

Cheryl breathed a sigh of relief. "I'm so glad that went as well as it did, but am I awful for also being glad to be gone?"

Lincoln chucked. "Definitely not. That was a stressful experience."

"And uncomfortable. Very uncomfortable."

Lincoln raised his eyebrows. "I couldn't tell you felt that way at all."

She shrugged. "Experience being in uncomfortable situations has led to excellent acting skills."

Lincoln wondered if she was referring to work, then decided to ask. It seemed like a question that wouldn't result in her returning to her earlier, angry self. He wanted to see if she'd open up further to him.

"What do you mean?" he said as they approached the next house.

She waved a hand in the air. "Oh, you know, doctor appointments for your kids where the doctor doesn't think you know what you're talking about. Or visiting an old friend who has changed so much where you're not compatible any longer. Or even patients who talk and talk and talk when you have other people to check in. I'm good at hiding discomfort."

Lincoln nodded. "I've probably gotten pretty good at it too." Considering his career, it was necessary.

"*What?* You're not constantly in love with the very thing you're doing the very minute you're doing it?" Cheryl laughed as she knocked on the door. "You could have had me fooled. I had no idea you were this energetic."

"It's gotten worse as I've aged, not better."

"Aw, man, that's not fair." She gave a little stomp of her foot, then walked back to the street when no one answered.

Was she flirting? The grin she sent his way said yes, and he returned it enthusiastically. "But no," he said, "that back there wasn't as bad for me as it was for you."

"Chloe definitely helped you feel comfortable, didn't

she." It wasn't a question, but there was a teasing glint in her eye when she said it.

"Sure, I guess. I like card games."

Cheryl looked at him, studying his face, then she laughed. "You didn't notice! You didn't notice a thing. I can't believe it."

"Notice what?"

"Never mind. I'm not going to draw your attention to something you're so oblivious to."

Lincoln frowned, trying to figure out what Cheryl was talking about. Nothing came to mind, and as they knocked on the last door, he started pestering her to tell him what she'd noticed. She refused, though. No one answered there either. He could tell she was grateful for that.

Lincoln's heart swelled with warmth when Cheryl said, "Let's go back for lunch." Somehow, over the course of the last few hours, she'd started saying "we and us" instead of "I and me." It both excited him and filled him with dread.

But maybe this time would be different. Maybe a relationship would actually go somewhere.

Assuming Cheryl actually wanted that. For all he knew, she was just warming up to the idea of being *friends*, and nothing more.

The walk back was fairly silent, both lost in their thoughts. Lincoln was pretty sure Cheryl needed the quiet, and he wanted time to process the fact that he might—just might—be opening his heart to yet another woman.

Could he handle that?

He wasn't sure. All he knew was this woman was special, and he didn't want to let her slip through his fingers for a second time.

Maybe the first time didn't count. Maybe anyone else

would say their first date hadn't happened because they weren't ready for it.

And maybe both of those things were true. Still, Lincoln found himself wanting to be on Cheryl's good side, despite the possibility that he'd get hurt again.

Thoughts still on his mind, Lincoln dug through the fridge while Cheryl retreated to her room, but when his gaze landed on her Dr Peppers and he remembered the googly eyes in his wallet, a grin crossed his face.

He knew exactly what he had to do.

CHAPTER 11

*C*heryl got up from the bed when she heard Lincoln rummaging through the fridge. No way was she going to let him make food for her again—she didn't want that to become a pattern during the rest of the vacation. She'd help him so he wouldn't feel like she was taking advantage of his generosity.

When she entered the kitchen, Lincoln glanced up from where he had bread laid out. "I figured something easy was in order. Do you like peanut butter and jelly sandwiches?"

A sandwich—that was easy. "Who doesn't?"

"Lots of people, actually."

"Fair enough. I can make my own, though."

Lincoln shrugged, stepping to the side so she could take over with her food. Though they were several inches apart, the entire half of Cheryl's body nearest him jumped to alertness. It felt like he was a magnet and she metal—something strong seemed to be pulling her to him, and she wasn't sure if she had the power to resist anymore.

Cheryl turned to face him, placing a hand on the counter, and opened her mouth to say something. But what? It wasn't as if she could just come out and ask him if he felt the same pull. No, that was way too forward.

Lincoln put down his butter knife, meeting her gaze. Neither of them said anything. They just stood there, looking at each other. Cheryl's heart raced at the intensity in his brown eyes, and she longed to grab him and pull his head down to hers. But despite the urge to close the distance between them, she was now fighting the desire to step away, too. To calm things down, to back off, especially if he wasn't okay with a relationship developing.

The fact that he still hadn't said something made it obvious either his thoughts were as far from hers as they could get or he wasn't ready for things to go that way.

Cheryl finally turned back to finish making her sandwich. He must think she was such a freak. What was wrong with her? Why couldn't she just say what was on her mind?

Then she remembered. He still hadn't told her why he'd stood her up. For all she knew, he was embarrassed about it. And for all she knew, he had a reason to be.

No, it was better to let him go at his own pace. As infuriating as that might be.

Cheryl finished making her sandwich, then put it on the table and turned to open the fridge. She jumped, hand flying to her chest, then laughed. Googly eyes had been attached to all of her diet Dr Peppers. She pulled one out and turned to Lincoln.

"You did this?"

"Did what?" He took a big bite of his sandwich, eyes wide, looking as innocent as he possibly could, and Cheryl couldn't help it—she laughed again.

He'd pulled a prank on her! And no, it wasn't the same thing as dipping her hair in ink, but it was close. Either he viewed her like a little sister—which she hoped wasn't the case—or he actually *liked* her.

Please don't be the sister thing.

She couldn't handle that. Not when she was developing feelings for him. Or rediscovering them.

Cheryl began eating her sandwich and drinking her Dr Pepper, enjoying how the eyes moved as she lifted the bottle to her lips, then set it back down again.

Lincoln cleared his throat and fiddled with his now-empty paper plate. Cheryl could tell he wanted to talk, and her palms immediately began sweating.

Instead of giving her the much-needed and much-deserved explanation, though, he said, "Tell me about life after high school graduation."

Ugh. Really? The one thing she *didn't* want to talk about. Mainly because it had all happened because of him. She would never have married that idiot if she hadn't been broken. She sighed. There had to be a way to tell the story without making it obvious her bad decisions happened as a direct result of her getting stood up.

"I got a boyfriend right around the time we graduated high school." Technically, a couple of months before graduation, but again, she didn't want Lincoln to suspect he'd had anything to do with it. "He wasn't the best guy, as you've probably guessed by now. But he was so sweet and made all sorts of promises, and I honestly believed I was in love."

She dropped her forehead to the table. "I was so young and naive. I still can't believe I actually thought I was ready to get married." Just to make sure Lincoln didn't misunderstand her, she raised her head and said, "A lot of people *are* ready at a young age. I was not one of them."

And frankly, neither was her ex. 'Course, he'd gotten worse, not better, over the years. Who knew at what point in his life he'd hit his prime. It hadn't happened while they were married.

"I'm sorry you went through that," Lincoln said, putting a hand on hers.

And there was that spark again. Did he feel it? She met his gaze, once more seeing the intense expression in his eyes. A twitterpated feeling nearly overwhelmed her, and she wondered if he wanted—was going to—kiss her.

No, not right after eating peanut butter and jelly sandwiches!

She tried to tell herself to knock it off. After all, hadn't she dreamed of kissing this man hundreds, if not thousands, of times?

"Was he ever abusive?" Lincoln asked, and Cheryl breathed a sigh of relief. No peanut butter kisses for them.

"Not physically, no. But my emotions were destroyed after I left him. It took a really long time to want to open up to someone again, but by then, the kids kept me busy. My whole life surrounds them."

"Maybe it doesn't need to?"

Despite how cautiously he'd said it, she still stiffened. "What do you mean?"

"Just that it sounds like you've always put them first. They're older now–they're learning to spread their own wings. Maybe it's time for you to put yourself first now. Just for a while. You deserve happiness too."

His explanation soothed her annoyance a little bit, but not enough to keep her from asking, "What about you? *You're* still single."

He smiled. "You can be happy and single, you know."

Cheryl couldn't help but wonder at that. Lincoln did seem well-adjusted, but to her, the ultimate pinnacle of happiness would be a wonderful marriage to a loving spouse.

She hadn't gotten that the first try. Was she ready to give it another go? And if so, would Lincoln be the one? Could she trust him with her heart?

Cheryl wasn't sure, but seeing his work ethic and how much he cared for others had done weird things to her resolution to dislike him.

Lincoln sighed, leaning back in his chair and putting his hands behind his head, and Cheryl tucked her own hands in her lap, already missing the contact.

"I've been in Hawaii for two days," he said, "and I still haven't been to the beach yet."

Cheryl blinked. "You're joking. How is that *possible*?"

He shrugged. "I knew I'd get plenty of time, so after I arrived, I settled myself in, then explored the yard. I almost caught a gecko."

Cheryl chuckled. Once a boy, always a boy. She still couldn't believe he hadn't gone to the beach yet, though. Utah had lots of sand dunes full of the softest sand you'd ever experience, and it had a salt lake—one of the only places on the planet that did—and it had shores, but it didn't have waves rolling against those shores, pounding relaxation into your mind with every crash.

He continued. "The next day, I discovered I had a visitor, and then the earthquake happened, and you know the rest." He sent her a grin, got to his feet, and started cleaning up. "You've already been, though, right?"

"Of course I have. It was the first thing I did when I got here."

He concentrated on putting the lid back on the peanut butter, then turned and sent her a quick glance. "Want to go with me now?"

Cheryl's heart warmed at his hesitation. How cautiously he asked, as if he thought she'd run screaming if he said it too forwardly. "A walk to the beach sounds great," she said.

She couldn't believe he'd actually asked her. What would snobby Whitney from high school say if she saw them? They were in Hawaii. Together. About to take a stroll to the beach. And no, they hadn't *come* together, but that didn't lessen the impact of the event that was about to take place.

Cheryl's head swam at everything that had happened in the short time since she'd arrived. Maybe her mom had been right to arrange everything because Cheryl's vacation was finally taking a turn for the better.

Cheryl and Lincoln headed out. She was extra aware of where her hands were in relation to his. He didn't seem to feel the same pressure, though, because he frequently pointed out things she hadn't noticed on their previous walks. Like, the massive spider webs. And the way vines covered an abandoned structure. And the many, many, many fences made of volcanic rock. How had Cheryl not noticed that last one? There were thousands of them, which made complete sense, given the sheer volume of volcanic rock on the island.

Her thoughts kept going to their hands, though. Maybe Lincoln *was* feeling the pressure. Maybe that was why he was distracting both of them so much.

Or maybe he thought she'd run if he was too forward.

Cheryl checked her body language. Yup, that had to be it. Her arms were stiff, her gait not relaxed in the slightest. She'd gotten so uptight over the years! But if she concentrated on relaxing too much, he'd definitely notice that too.

Ugh. Ridiculous.

The more they walked and chatted about random things, the more Cheryl realized something. Lincoln's personality hadn't changed all that much. Sure, he was more mature and experienced now, but he still had the boyish enthusiasm and energy that just didn't ever seem to wane.

Compared to Cheryl, his energy levels put him at toddler still. But looking at him, there wasn't anything infantile about him. And the expressions he sent her—tenderness, cautious optimism—made her knees weak. Could it be possible that he was falling for her too?

They arrived at the beach, and Cheryl showed Lincoln the spot where she'd seen dolphins the day before. The two of them settled in to watch the waves and hopefully catch sight of the dolphins again.

She hoped they'd open up and have another serious conversation, but the setting didn't feel right. The beach wasn't very busy, but there were several people nearby, and conversation remained light.

She sighed. It would have to do.

An hour later, they decided to check if the City of Refuge was open. Cheryl had read about it in the airport and wanted to see the area that many native Hawaiians still believed was sacred.

Luck was on their side—the park was open. The man who let them in admitted he lived nearby and had gotten bored, so decided to open up for other bored people.

"Thank you so much," Cheryl said, grateful her desire would come to fruition.

They'd only been inside for a moment when Lincoln sent her a curious expression. "I love visiting historical places, but I have to admit I'd never heard of this one."

"Me neither," she said. "I read about it while waiting at the airport. It's pretty cool."

She proceeded to tell him how multiple chiefs had been buried there, and as such, the grounds were sacred.

"Battles weren't fought here—none of the tribal leaders dared do it, lest they be punished by God." Cheryl took on the role of tour guide, showing Lincoln the huts that had been erected to look like ones that might have been used hundreds of years earlier. Together, they discovered a massive wall meant to separate an ancient village from the gravesite, both of them in awe that the people had been able to build it at all.

Cheryl continued her mini lecture as they walked on to the next thing.

"Back then, because of the sacred nature of the City of Refuge, if someone broke a law, they'd swim here for safety. The elder here would help them basically repent— get a second chance on life—and they'd swim back home. When they got there, the people accepted that they'd received that second chance, and their sins that would usually result in death would be pardoned."

"What sorts of sins are we talking about?" Lincoln asked.

"Oh, you know, the usual. Looking at the chief, talking to him, or touching any of his possessions. That was if you were a guy. It was a lot harder to be women—they weren't allowed to eat in the presence of men or even cook for male villagers. Again, if they did, they were put to death."

Lincoln's eyebrows went up. "Wow. Strict laws."

Cheryl nodded. "But the City of Refuge protected

anyone who was able to reach it. And like I said, all sins were forgiven after they went home." It was quite a swim from where the village had been to the City of Refuge. Making it at all was a feat in and of itself.

Lincoln stepped closer to Cheryl and pointed out a goat drinking from a stream. "Think it's wild?"

"Probably. Just like yesterday's chickens."

He chuckled. "Still haven't gotten over that, huh?"

She shook her head. "Never."

Lincoln's hand brushed hers, and when she didn't shy away, he took it in his own, intertwining their fingers.

Cheryl about died. She nearly asked for someone to bury her next to the chiefs because surely, she was in heaven or about to go there. It felt so good, so complete, so right to be holding his hand.

And not just that, it felt . . . She wasn't sure what else. She'd never experienced such euphoria with anyone before, not even her ex-husband.

"For the record," Lincoln whispered. "You can cook for me any time and I won't put you to death." His grin was big.

"We both know it's too late for me," she said. "I've already eaten in front of you."

They both laughed, then Lincoln sobered up. "We probably shouldn't make light of their customs. Things were very different then. Life was a lot harder."

Cheryl nodded. "And women were regarded as possessions by more than one culture."

Lincoln turned to her, taking her other hand in his and stepping closer. "We've learned respect over the years."

She couldn't look away from him, his expression was so intense. She'd almost forgotten what he'd said, and she definitely couldn't come up with a response. He searched her eyes, looking for something. She returned his gaze with courage she didn't know she had, trying to share her feelings without words. When he found—or didn't find—what he was looking for, he pressed his forehead against hers.

"Let's keep going," he said quietly, his voice thick.

They continued their tour, and despite her confusion over why he'd pulled away, Cheryl pretended nothing had happened between them, pointing out the fascinating tools the villagers had used and what they were used for.

Through it all, Lincoln didn't let go of her hand. Maybe, then, he'd found what he was looking for, but didn't yet know how to proceed. The fact that he hadn't released her showed he felt the same—that he wanted to maintain contact with her.

That knowledge was comforting to her, and the City of Refuge would forever go down in her mind as one of the best places on the face of the earth. Her heart was opening up, inviting Lincoln in, promising him he could find refuge there. Promising she wouldn't ever do anything to hurt him.

Of course, she couldn't actually say those sorts of things. She didn't have the courage just yet. But they were on her mind and in her heart all the same.

CHAPTER 12

*D*espite his earlier words, Lincoln wanted nothing more than to cook a fantastic dinner for Cheryl. If she hadn't had breakfast in a long time, she probably hadn't ever had someone cook for her. At least, not a man. He doubted the idea had ever even occurred to her ex.

As soon as they were back, Lincoln started marinating the meat and sifting through the possible options for sides. He couldn't wait.

If he was being honest with himself, he couldn't wait for whatever might happen after dinner. She'd been fine with him holding her hand. At the beach, when he'd almost taken it for the first time, she'd been tense and even skittish. But at the City of Refuge, she'd relaxed and opened up. Maybe it was because she'd adopted the role of tour guide and felt engaged. Or maybe it was the calm, peaceful feeling that surrounded the park. Whatever it was, he was grateful it had happened.

He decided, as he started cooking the meat, that he was going to kiss her that evening.

At least, that was the plan. Her skittish side might

return after he told her about his parents, which was something that definitely needed to happen over dinner. He just hoped things would go well, that she'd understand what his situation had been, and would remain open to him.

And then, kissing time.

He practically danced while throwing veggies into a frying pan on the stove top.

"You're cheerful," Cheryl said.

"Mmhmm. I enjoy cooking."

She stepped beside him, looking up at him incredulously. "Are you serious?"

He shrugged. "We're rare, but we do exist."

"I can't believe it. Wow. I'm in for a treat."

He held up a finger. "Only if it turns out. I never said I was a good cook."

She laughed, gave his arm a squeeze that sent shivers up into his shoulder and across his back, and asked, "Is there anything I can do?"

"Sure. Grate some cheese?"

She nodded, grabbing the things she'd need and settling at the table to get to work. Lincoln had planned most of the meal the day before, pulling things out of the freezer, and he was glad now that he had. This was one of his best recipes. If she didn't like it . . . well, she probably wasn't the woman for him.

That thought sobered him for a moment. If the last fifteen years of deciding he wasn't meant to get married proved true, she wasn't the woman for him anyway.

But maybe—maybe—he'd been wrong about all of that. Maybe he just hadn't met the right woman. Or met her again, in this case.

Only time would tell. But he started hoping against all

odds that she would be perfect for him and that someone higher up would agree.

It took him two hours to cook dinner, but at Cheryl's first bite, he knew she loved it.

"This is sublime," she said about the bacon-wrapped sirloin. "So juicy and tender and those flavors . . . I'm going to die and go to heaven right now."

"I hope not," he said with a chuckle. "That would defeat the purpose of all the work I put into it."

"I still can't believe you enjoy cooking."

He studied her face for a moment. "There are a lot of things you don't know about me."

She lowered her fork, and the expression of anticipation on her face told him she knew what he was about to bring up. She waited patiently, and he set his fork down too.

"Cheryl . . . A couple of hours before you came to pick me up that night, there was a big storm. Do you remember it?"

She frowned, probably thinking back. "Not really."

"It was the same storm that knocked over the tree in the field across from the high school."

That, she remembered. He could tell by her expression. "Okay, yes."

"My parents were heading back from eating lunch with friends when the rain started. It was one of the biggest storms we'd had in a long time." He closed his eyes, the memories flashing through his mind. "My dad's car hydroplaned, and he lost control. He spun out, flipped around, and hit the barrier between north and southbound traffic on the freeway."

Cheryl gasped, and Lincoln opened his eyes. She had

a hand at her mouth and was staring at him with an expression of horror. "What happened?"

He gave a half shrug. "They were life flighted to the regional hospital."

"And then . . .?"

He realized he was clenching his fork and forced himself to relax his hold on it. He didn't even remember picking it up again. "They were in the hospital for months. Dad pulled out better than Mom. She was in the ICU for over five weeks. We didn't think she would make it."

"But she did?" Cheryl looked hopeful.

Lincoln felt the backs of his eyes burning. "Yes, she did. But . . . the damage she'd sustained was too much, and she wasn't ever the same again." He paused, clearing his throat. "And because she wasn't the same, neither was my dad."

His mind flitted back to the weeks, months, and even years after everything had happened. To the prayers they'd given, the meals that had been shared with them, the tears shed. To his father drifting away after his mom's personality—her essence, what made her *her*—didn't return. How Joshua had come back from being deployed to take over helping the family, but he'd been gone so long their younger sisters refused to bond with him. And how Lincoln had been forced to grow up faster than he'd been ready to.

"It was a hard time," he whispered. "A very hard time." He cleared his throat again, willing himself not to cry. It had been years since he'd felt this emotional about the accident. "My dad eventually came around again, but by then, my younger sisters were in high school and I was off getting my PhD as a physical therapist."

Cheryl reached across the table and gave his hand a

squeeze. "I'm so sorry, Lincoln. I never knew."

He could tell she was appalled about that. "The school kept it quiet. I didn't tell anyone except my close friends. But you remember all those absences of mine?"

She slowly shook her head. "I didn't notice. The next day, I transferred out of all of the classes we had together."

He blinked. He didn't remember that. Of course, he'd not been in school much the months after his parents' accident, and he was back with Brittany by that point, but still. "Suffice to say," he continued, "it was very hard to graduate on time. I was a good student before the accident, and my teachers were lenient with me. Otherwise, I wouldn't have made it."

Cheryl shook her head. "I'm so sorry," she repeated. He could tell she didn't know what else to say.

"It's all right." He reached over and gave her hand a squeeze. She might have thought he was done, but now that the cork had been pulled out, he had a whole lot more to say, including the bit about Brittany. "I got back with Brittany, my ex-girlfriend, right after the accident. She promised to tell you what happened, but I'm thinking she never did."

"I knew you got back with her. She told me she needed to talk to me, but I thought she wanted to rub in your relationship, and I told her never to approach me again. I mean, she *was* friends with Whitney."

Lincoln rolled his eyes. "Whitney . . .. They were only friends because they were both cheerleaders. Brittney was as sweet as they come. Charitable too."

Cheryl looked like she had her doubts, but she didn't press the matter except to say, "Guilty by association, I guess."

Lincoln nodded. "Either way, I was very distracted for a while. But Cheryl, please believe me when I say I'm sorry for all of that. If I'd only known Brittany hadn't been able to get the message to you, I would have done everything in my power to make sure you knew what happened. But I shouldn't have assumed. I should have delivered it myself."

Cheryl squeezed his hand. "You don't have anything to apologize for. I only wish I hadn't spent so many years feeling bitter and angry and spurned . . ." She sighed, and he saw the regret in her eyes. "So many wasted years."

His earlier guesses were proving to be correct—that one missed date had caused her a lot of turmoil and problems with insecurity. Her skittishness earlier was a direct result of that, and he had no doubt that she'd been that way where all men were concerned.

Guilt hit him hard in the pit of the stomach, and he swore that if he ever had the chance to redeem himself, he'd take it.

"Is there a priest nearby?" he asked.

Cheryl blinked. "Excuse me?"

"I'm near the City of Refuge. Maybe I could get the priest to help me find a second chance at life. For the wrongs I've committed against you."

Cheryl's cheeks pinked up, and Lincoln's gaze dropped to her lips. They'd only had a few bites each, but he was sorely tempted to push the entire dinner aside.

"Let's finish eating before it gets cold," Cheryl said, seeming to know where his thoughts had gone. "It would be very sad for all of your work to go to waste."

He agreed, and they finished off their food, enjoying a scoop of ice cream as dessert before cleaning up and heading to the couches for a movie.

CHAPTER 13

Cheryl still couldn't believe Lincoln's story. Well, she *did* believe him, but she had a hard time understanding why she hadn't heard about it. Not even an ounce of a stray rumor had reached her ears.

But looking back at how much of a shut-in she'd become after that, how much she avoided other students in general, was it really that much of a surprise? Her best friend had been a year older than her, and after she graduated, Cheryl never quite replaced her. No one else was there to help her feel grounded in the local goings-on of the school. And the fact that she transferred out of all of the classes she'd shared with Lincoln, and his family asking the school to keep things quiet . . . No wonder she never heard anything.

But still . . . Cheryl felt like a part of her was off—like she'd missed something huge for not having known all of that about his parents.

One thing was certain, though. The events of that day had scarred him just as much as they had her. But he'd somehow managed to overcome them—to move on, to possibly even be a stronger, better person for them.

What about *her*? She'd gone off and married the first guy to show "love" toward her, had two kids with him, then refused to have more when she realized doing so wouldn't fix her relationship. Even after recognizing she was in a dead-end marriage to a dead-beat and abusive man, she stuck it out as long as possible.

Too long, given her current state of mind.

Ugh.

Cheryl couldn't dwell on herself for long after hearing his story, though. He'd endured far more heartache than she had, and hers was mostly self-inflicted.

Shame made her cheeks burn. She was so pathetic.

She took a breath and closed her eyes as Lincoln set up a movie for them to watch. Destructive thoughts were what had gotten her into her failed marriage in the first place. She *had* to stop making herself feel guilt and shame over something that had happened years earlier.

It was time *she* healed.

Lincoln joined her at the couch, sitting close enough for their thighs and arms to touch, and Cheryl felt her whole body both awaken and relax at the contact. Tingles flared to life everywhere they touched. His long-awaited explanation seemed to have unlocked the part of her she'd been holding back.

The previews started playing, and rather than ask him to skip them, she turned to him and asked, "What happened with your mother?"

"She passed away a few years ago when she aspirated on her food."

A wave of horror flooded across Cheryl. "How awful!"

"Yeah, it was brutal for her."

"I can't even imagine. And for you and your siblings too."

Lincoln took her hand, bringing it up and placing a kiss on the back of it, his chocolate-brown eyes not leaving her face. Cheryl's insides turned to goo, and she was grateful she was propped up against him. The tingles burned stronger.

"I hope I don't sound like an awful person when I say this," Lincoln said, "but her passing was a blessing and a relief. Like I said, she never was the same—her brain had suffered so much damage that I couldn't even tell she was my mom anymore. She'd been paralyzed, and had so many health problems. Her doctors believed she was in constant pain, and judging by how often she scowled, I think they were right. It wasn't a good situation for her, and I know she feels a lot of relief wherever she is now."

Tears pricked the backs of Cheryl's eyes. "I'm so sorry you experienced all of that."

His Adam's apple bobbed as he swallowed, and he didn't meet her gaze. "Me too."

"But things are better now? For you all?"

He nodded. "Both of my sisters are married and have kids. They're happy—they married well, and their spouses worship them. Plus, both in-laws have mothers who have pretty much adopted my sisters. And Joshua, my older brother, is engaged." He glanced at Cheryl. "His first wife died of cancer a few years ago."

Cheryl shook her head. "Poor Joshua."

"I know. He's pretty happy now, though."

So much heartache for one family to endure. "And your dad?"

"He's remarried now and is also happy."

It wouldn't have taken a genius to notice how many

times Lincoln mentioned the word "happy" in relation to his family. "What about *you*?"

"I'm happy too."

But was he? Cheryl didn't want to question that—she felt like it would be rude to assume he was hiding his true feelings. She couldn't help but wonder, though. He was the only one out of his siblings who hadn't ever married. Was he avoiding marriage to keep himself safe from more possible heartache? Could she ask without seeming like she was prying?

"What did you do after graduation? Did you date anyone?"

Lincoln snorted. "Yes. None of my relationships went well, though."

Was it because of his own emotional baggage or something else?

Cheryl rubbed a circle on the back of Lincoln's hand, aware that the movie had reached the disk menu and the music was cycling over and over again. "We don't need to talk about it if you don't want to."

Lincoln shifted his position so he was facing her better, and she did the same thing, her stomach flipping at their closeness and the intimacy of the position. It would be so easy to lean forward and kiss him.

"I want to," he said. "I haven't talked to anyone about . . . my relationships in a very long time."

It felt like he'd nearly said something else. What? "Not even family?"

He waved a hand in the air. "They gave up a long time ago. I'm over forty, after all." He gave a bark of a laugh. "They probably think I'm gay."

Cheryl giggled. "They obviously don't know you very

well if they think that. I mean, you *were* the guy in high school who always had a girlfriend."

He grinned at her. "What can I say, it was tough."

Cheryl laughed. "Apparently." She sobered up, wanting to help him get whatever was on his chest off of it. "What happened with Brittany?"

Lincoln groaned and rubbed the back of his neck with the hand not holding hers. "We dated through college. I asked her to marry me. She said no."

Sensing he wanted to say more, she asked, "Did she mention why?"

He grunted. "Oh, yes. More than once." He raised his voice to sound like a woman. "'Dating you is so much fun, and I'm so glad I was able to help you out when things went down with your family, but I don't think I love you as much as you love me.'"

He looked at Cheryl. "We discussed it multiple times. I thought she was wrong—why continue dating me for so long, otherwise? But nothing changed her mind. In the end, I realized how pathetic it was for me to continue trying to convince someone to marry me who didn't actually want me."

It was as if a dam somewhere in Lincoln's mind exploded because he started talking quickly.

"She was my first serious relationship. My next girlfriend and I dated for a couple of years. I proposed around the one-year mark. She also said no. Though, it wasn't a solid no. It was almost always, "Not now." At first, she led me to believe it was because she wanted a promotion before getting married or she wanted to switch departments—always something to do with her career. But she always put me off when I asked. I tried with her for a full year before realizing she was never going to say yes. After a week of wrestling out in my mind, I finally walked away. She didn't even cry."

"At least *you* broke up with *her*."

He gave Cheryl a sad smile. "There's that, I suppose. After her, I didn't date again for a few years. I focused on finishing up my doctorate. Once that happened, and I got over the stress of finals and tests and had my degrees, I gave it one more try with a woman named Taylor.

"She and I dated for another two years. By the end of the two years, I had opened my rehab center and was settled in. She said yes when I proposed. I almost couldn't believe it—finally, I found a woman who was as madly in love with me as I was with her. I should have known it wouldn't work out."

"What happened?"

"She decided she couldn't bear to settle down in Utah. She moved back to Kansas where—" And his voice rose in pitch again ""—nothing obstructs your views of the sky.'"

Cheryl blinked. "The *mountains*? She broke up with you over *mountains*? That's the most ridiculous thing I've ever heard."

Lincoln laughed. "There had to be other reasons, but she never shared them with me."

"It wasn't as if you could follow her to Kansas and live there—not after having just set up your practice."

"Exactly. Even if I'd wanted to—which I didn't, I actually like Utah—I couldn't have. I had too much money at stake. It would have cost millions if I'd abandoned my practice."

Cheryl blinked. *Millions?* How had he found that much money?

He seemed to know what was on her mind. "I'm part of a much larger company. I own and run the facility I set up, but there are five others across the state. They helped with the initial funding, chose the location, gave me their name, and they take a portion of my profits each month. A rather large portion, I might add. My share of the profits will increase once I've repaid them in full."

Cheryl nodded. That made sense. "How long have you been in business there?"

He leaned back, thinking. "I'm coming up on my ten-year mark here soon."

"Wow. That's a long time."

"It is. It was rough when Taylor broke up with me, but I'm so glad I stayed. This is where I belong."

"In Hawaii?" Cheryl sent him a teasing grin, which he returned.

"Right now? Definitely." He picked up her other hand in his, and not meeting her gaze, rubbed his thumbs across the back of her hands, setting off little fires in her skin. "Are we good now? With what happened back in high school?"

Cheryl hesitated for a moment before answering, wanting to search her heart and her feelings. "Yes. We are."

The warmth that flooded her chest when she said those words confirmed it for her. In them, she felt the forgiveness she'd extended to him. They'd both suffered a great deal, and it was time for that to end. She could tell that having that much rejection had really done something to him. To his heart, to his confidence where love was concerned. She hoped she'd have the opportunity to make things better.

Lincoln released her hands, then trailed his own up and down her arms slowly, tingles and sparks following his movement, making her ache to increase their contact. His gaze was on hers, his expression serious.

When his eyes dropped to her lips, she knew he wanted to kiss her. Yet, he hesitated. Was he waiting for more of a sign from her? More confirmation that she wasn't going to run?

Yes, Cheryl thought, *he was*. She realized she'd clasped her hands tightly in her lap, her arms rigid, and she forced herself to relax them. She wanted nothing more than to kiss him right then. And so, not hesitating, she put her hands on his shoulders and pulled him closer.

Lincoln grinned, settling his hands around her waist, moving in. Instead of going for her mouth, though, he grazed her cheekbone with his lips, nibbling lightly, then trailing kisses down her cheek, to her chin, and across to her other cheekbone. Cheryl sighed, closing her eyes, enjoying the explosion of warmth and butterflies and shivers that nearly consumed her.

When he finally made his way to her lips, she was ready for it. She wrapped her arms around his neck, pulling him in as closely as she could, all thoughts of the repeating DVD menu forgotten.

She forgot everything else too—the hurt she'd experienced over the years, the bitterness she'd felt, and the tears she'd shed. With that kiss, she recognized she'd truly forgiven him. Now, it felt silly. It felt trivial, in comparison to what he'd experienced. He'd never say what she'd gone through had been easy, but she *felt* it and knew it was.

Lincoln pulled away for a moment before placing several kisses on her lips, then breathing, "Thank you, Helen."

Cheryl blinked, surprised for a moment at the mention

of her mother, then chuckled, turning her head to the side as he kissed her cheek and jawline. "Most of my mom's conniving plans actually turn out . . . but this one has been the best of them yet."

Lincoln rubbed Cheryl's arms again, his expression warm. "Definitely the best."

They kissed for several minutes more, but the sound of the front door opening interrupted them, and rather than let the DVD menu continue running, they decided to start the movie instead of risking Susan or Tom coming downstairs to find out why the TV had been left on.

Cheryl nestled up against Lincoln's side, and he wrapped his arm around her, pulling her in tight.

They planned to watch the show, but Cheryl didn't remember most of it. Lincoln stole kiss after kiss until they put their focus on each other entirely for the remainder of the movie.

It was the most wonderful night Cheryl remembered having. A delicious home-cooked dinner, a heart-to-heart conversation, and the best kisses she'd ever shared.

Yes. Thank you, Mom.

CHERYL WOKE UP SLOWLY, warmth filling her from her fingertips to toes, and she stretched, remembering the night before. Lincoln . . . He'd been amazing. She brushed her lips, still able to feel his mouth against hers.

She shivered, just thinking about it. Dang it, that man was hot.

She rolled to a sitting position and checked her texts. She had one from an unknown number.

Hey, just wanted to tell you that tonight was the most fun I've had in a long time. Thank you for sharing the evening with me. ♥

Lincoln must have gotten her number from her mom. Cheryl saved it, then debated answering right then or not. She'd be seeing him again in a few minutes—her body yearned for that to happen now. But not answering him would possibly make him feel weird about texting in the first place. Maybe. She didn't know. She opted to answer just in case, playing with the idea of flirting with him by saying something like, "My lips miss yours," but decided simple was better.

Thank you too. I really enjoyed myself. ♥

Ready to get started on what would hopefully be a day full of Lincoln, Cheryl hurried to get dressed. She passed him in the hall, and despite the fact that she hadn't brushed her teeth yet, he still insisted on giving her a good morning kiss. He enveloped her with his arms, pulling her so tight she almost couldn't breathe, then smothered her face with little pecks before kissing her lips soundly.

Oh, man, this guy was so good. She melted against him, arms encircling his neck, wondering at the fact that she'd *kissed*—was *kissing*—Lincoln Tanner, student body president.

Her teenage self went absolutely wild. Her adult self was still shocked.

"Breakfast?" he mumbled after finally releasing her.

"Sure. I'll cook it this time," she said.

"I'll help."

"Deal. Now would you please let me go brush my disgusting teeth?"

He chuckled. "Kissing you was the farthest thing from disgusting ever. You could skip brushing your teeth for the rest of our lives and I wouldn't notice."

Outwardly, she play-scoffed, but inwardly, she celebrated. *Our* lives? Was he really thinking that far into the future? Oh, she hoped so! "That's gross, Lincoln. I'd probably grow mold on my teeth."

"Oh, man. Thanks for the visual."

She swatted him playfully. "It's your fault—you're the one who put the idea there."

He winked at her, then gave her a little peck on the cheek. "Go wash your nasty teeth. I'll start breakfast."

She laughed, loving how easily he joked with her and how readily he seemed to get her sense of humor. It was so refreshing, so wonderful. Her ex had thought her jokes stupid. He was all about pillow fights, burping, tickling, and passing gas. Anything that wasn't physical in some way was completely lost on him.

When she got out of the bathroom, Lincoln was filling a glass pan with the ingredients for a breakfast casserole.

"Mmmm . . ." she said. "I love breakfast casseroles."

"Me too. They're easy, fast, and best of all, they give lots of leftovers."

She grinned. "Leftovers are great. I thought I was going to cook most of it, though."

He sent her a wicked grin. "I guess you'll owe me."

She wrapped her arms around his waist and placed a kiss on his mouth. "I guess I will."

Once the food was in the oven, the two of them sat on the couch and planned out their day.

"Tom was telling me about a beach made entirely of black sand," Lincoln said. "Want to visit it?"

"Is it nearby?" Cheryl asked. "The roads are still closed."

"They were able to finish the construction late last night. Tom came down to let us know."

"Oh, that's great." Cheryl sent him a sly grin. "Guess you'll be finding a hotel now. Hope the rest of your vacation goes well."

Lincoln laughed, then said, "Wait, you're joking, right?"

"Of course I am. You're not going anywhere."

Instead of the response she expected, the serious expression stayed on his face. "I hope not."

What did he mean by that? Was he expecting another emergency to happen that would separate them? Or a call from his family? Or . . . Instead of letting it plague her all day, Cheryl decided to ask him. "What do you mean, you hope not?" She sat up and faced him squarely. "Are you sick or something? Cancer?"

Lincoln blinked. "No, thank goodness. I just . . ." He trailed off, shook his head, then pointed to the notepad she held. "Let's plan to see the black-sand beach and then finish up at Volcanoes National Park."

She decided not to press the matter. She knew he had something on his mind, and she hoped he'd share it with her at some point, but for now, it could rest. "And eat lunch and dinner somewhere along the way? Isn't Volcanoes National Park best at night, when you can see the glow of the lava?"

"Tom was saying there's plenty to do there before nightfall. We can eat dinner in the restaurant at the visitor center, go on some of the trails, spend time in the gift shop, then head to the volcano at sunset."

Cheryl's phone beeped with an incoming text message, and she woke the device to see who it was from. A smile spread across her face at the text from Jade.

"Give me a minute to answer this," she said.

Lincoln nodded, pulling out his own phone, his finger

swiping quickly across the screen as he wrote out a text to someone, and Cheryl read Jade's message.

Grandma told Jack and Jack told me n Xander that you n Dr. Lincoln are like dating now or something is that true?

He kissed me last night. I'll fill you in when I get back.

She put her phone away, wanting more than anything to have an in-depth conversation with her daughter who was finally starting to understand that a good crush was one of the best things in the world. That would have to wait, though. She turned back to Lincoln. "Ready?"

"Family back home?" he asked.

"Yes, my daughter, Jade."

He nodded, but didn't respond. His expression made Cheryl's stomach drop a little. He looked like he was trying to be casual about everything, but the mention of her daughter had him frowning slightly.

Please don't hold my kids against me. They were her entire life, and she couldn't leave them for anyone—not even him. But he didn't have children. He might not even want them. They hadn't discussed it the night before. Maybe there were other reasons the women didn't want to marry him. If they had wanted a family and he hadn't . . .

Knock it off, Cheryl. You're overreacting. He hasn't given you anything to believe he has something against kids. Just relax and enjoy yourself.

But still, Cheryl couldn't help but worry that he would end up breaking her heart all over again. This trip to Hawaii was turning out to be a lot of fun—especially the kissing part, with prospects of more kisses to come. But what would happen when they returned?

Even though she was having the time of her life, she was grateful for one thing—her mom was nearly done with physical therapy. If things went south, Cheryl wouldn't ever have to see Lincoln again.

Why was she already thinking about breaking up with him? Wasn't it enough to simply enjoy their time together? Yes. Yes, it was.

Tucking her negative thoughts aside, she turned to him and smiled. "Let's do this."

Relief washed over her when a genuine, eager grin split his face and he said, "Okay."

The two of them gathered things for the drive, then headed out.

CHAPTER 14

*L*incoln was really enjoying himself. Cheryl had truly opened up to him, and they'd laughed, shared kisses, and enjoyed the sights, sounds, and smells of the tropical island. The black sand was beautiful, dramatic, and fascinating, and they even saw a couple of large turtles in the shallow water by the shore.

They ate lunch at a different beach that had once been a major port in Hawaii—maybe a hundred years earlier. All that remained were huge, dramatic cement blocks, standing in the water where the ships used to drop anchor. The waves crashed against that cement and massive rocks in the ocean, and Cheryl told Lincoln that the area was known for large waves and a lot of injuries and even deaths as people attempted to surf there.

Lincoln didn't know what would make someone want to surf that beach—the waves crashed so heavily into the rocks and cement that it jolted his bones just watching. But it was definitely beautiful.

Once they'd had their fill of the ocean, they headed to Volcanoes National Park and went on a few hikes in the area. None of them gave a glimpse of the active volcano, but Lincoln assumed they wouldn't see much of it until the sun had gone down anyway.

They had dinner at the restaurant, and when the sun started dipping below the horizon, they headed to the main viewpoint. It took them a few minutes to reach the first scenic spot, and it was fairly crowded. Lincoln wanted some quiet time with Cheryl, so they hiked up to a higher area where they could be mostly alone.

The view was better there, but Lincoln could tell why people didn't go that way—the path was short and difficult and hard to find. Once at the top, he stepped behind her and put his arms around her waist, pulling her back against his chest. She relaxed there, practically melting in his embrace. He couldn't believe how good it felt to hold her.

Neither of them said anything as they watched the red glows swirl into the night air. Tom had been right—they couldn't see the actual lava, but that bright red was quite something. They weren't close enough to feel the heat, but Lincoln still couldn't believe he stood next to an actual volcano.

"It feels like I'm taking a step back through time," he whispered into her hair.

"Meaning?"

"An actual, active volcano. These just don't happen back home. Hardly anywhere on the planet, actually."

She chuckled. "And here I thought you were going to say something about being back in *high school* again."

He grinned. "I can see why you would think that. But no—I'm talking about the volcano one hundred percent. This is the sort of thing dinosaurs saw."

"So . . . romantic or is there too much science here?"

Lincoln, sensing a deeper question, turned her around. It was too dark to see much, but light from the stars and moon reflected off her bright eyes. He made sure he had her full attention—which wasn't hard to get, as his arms were tight around her—then lowered his mouth to hers.

Her lips were soft, warm, inviting. She breathed a sigh against him before raising her arms around his neck and returning the kiss. He pulled her in as tightly as he could, rushing to explore her face, neck, and ears before gently nibbling on her lips.

They kissed for several moments, then Cheryl turned, leaning her head against his chest.

"Definitely more romance than science," he said.

She chuckled. "Good."

Cheryl shifted, and he sensed she wanted to keep talking. He waited, enjoying the moment.

"This has been the best vacation ever. I'm sad it has to end."

He paused, then took her by the waist and pulled back so he could see her eyes again. "Things don't have to end between us when we go home."

Cheryl looked away, and Lincoln's heart twisted. He was giving himself to her completely and totally, but she seemed to be hesitating still. "I'm serious," he said, feeling like he was grasping at straws to convince her. "Why would it need to be different?"

"It doesn't need to be," she said. But her tone—artificially light, casual—said other things. She was nervous or hesitant about something.

He put his finger under her chin. "Cheryl, look at me." She did, and he said, "This is new to me too. Let's just take things a day at a time, okay? We can enjoy one another's time without getting too serious." Without freaking themselves out prematurely.

She took in a deep breath, let it out slowly, then nodded, giving him a smile that was barely visible in the darkness. But then she put her arms around his neck and pulled him in for another spine-tingling kiss, and he knew she was at least considering what he'd said.

Still, a little voice nagged at him not to fall for her faster than she was for him.

You haven't forgotten, have you? You're not meant to get married. That sort of happiness is reserved for other people.

He scowled at himself, then pushed the thought away and tightened his arms around the woman in front of him. He didn't know how she felt about him per se, but if her kisses said anything, she liked him as much as he liked her. Besides, anyone who could hold a grudge as long as she had was someone who could love just as fiercely. Which said good things—if she was as determined at loving him as she'd been at hating him, they'd be fine.

Cheryl was distant and quiet on the way home, though, and no matter what little argument or lecture he gave himself, he felt his heart putting up shields. *Protect yourself—just in case. Don't let her in too much or you'll be hurt.*

Another rejection would undo him. He didn't think he would survive one from her.

CHAPTER 15

*C*heryl's phone rang, vibrating in her hand as she was entering her bedroom. She'd just given Lincoln a kiss goodnight, he was already in his room, and she couldn't wait to hit the sack. But when she saw who was calling—her mom—she knew she had to take it. She dropped her things on her bed, shut her door, and whispered, "Hello?"

"Cheryl? Is that you? I can barely hear you."

"Yeah, it's me. Give me a second to go somewhere more private."

Cheryl had overheard a part of a phone conversation Lincoln had had with Joshua about a patient the other day, so she knew he'd be able to hear everything they said if she stuck around. No way was *that* happening.

While her mom waited, Cheryl left her room, quietly shutting the bedroom door behind her, then headed out through the kitchen and to the front porch. She'd walk to the beach. It was safe enough for her to do that, and she desperately needed some ocean time again.

"Okay, I'm outside now," she said at normal volume.

"I'm so glad you called—I *really* needed a talk with my mom. But it's so late back home! Why are you even up?"

"I could sense turmoil floating my way from Hawaii. There's no way a mom can sleep when she feels that one of her kids is upset. Are you having fun?"

"Of course I am—you already know we've kissed."

"And I couldn't be happier about that."

Cheryl smiled. "He's great." Her smile faded as her earlier doubts cropped up in her mind again. She sighed. "I don't know, Mom. Are we having a choir tour romance?"

"Huh?"

"Is this just a vacation fling? Will it actually go anywhere when we get home?"

"Why are you thinking thoughts like that? You've only been dating a few days."

It felt like so much longer than that. In both good ways and bad.

"Tell me your thoughts, honey," her mom said when she didn't answer. "Let's work through them."

"I've loved this vacation. It's exactly what I needed. But our relationship has really jumped forward, and fast. I don't know if he's good for me or if *I'm* good for *him*. I don't know if I want to date him." She was walking quickly, and her breath was coming in short gasps. "I mean, I've had a crush on this man for so many years. I realize now I never got over it. But what if I've built him up to be more than he is? What if he disappoints me? What if I find out we're completely incompatible? What if he hates my kids and doesn't want to have anything to do with a woman who was previously married, has stretch marks and loose skin from pregnancies still, and has the amount of baggage I have?"

"You don't think he'll like Xander and Jade?"

Cheryl wasn't surprised her mom picked up on that particular theme right away. Helen's grandkids were as important to Helen as they were to Cheryl, albeit in different ways.

"He acted weird earlier when he found out I had a text from Jade. Like, 'Oh, yeah . . . she has kids,' kinda weird. Do you know anything about him where children are concerned?"

Helen paused. "I don't, honey. I've never seen him with kids, he's never mentioned them, and no one else has. Which isn't a big surprise, given the age of most of the patients here. But you'd think a few of them would have grandkids coming to visit. I haven't seen any, other than my own."

"Maybe it's because he has an unspoken rule where they're concerned. Or because he's off-putting, and they can sense it the moment they step foot on the property, and it repels them before they can even enter the building."

"Except for Xander and Jade."

"We all know they have superpowers."

Helen chuckled. "Honey, I understand your concern, and obviously I share it. If he doesn't like your children, there's no point in dating him. It wouldn't ever go beyond just dating. And I don't believe someone who doesn't like kids will eventually come around—they might learn to tolerate other people's children, but Xander and Jade are too hands on for that. They need a dad who will love them nearly as much as you or I do."

Cheryl slumped down on the volcanic rock near the beach, grateful that her mother understood her dilemma so perfectly. What had she ever done to deserve such a wonderful mom?

"What do I do?"

Helen chuckled. "Nothing. There isn't anything you *can* do. Enjoy the rest of your time there, continue getting to know him, and relax. Nothing will happen until you come home, anyway."

Cheryl rubbed her forehead, watching the waves. "I don't know if I can do that, Mom. I'm such a planner—I always know what to expect from my future. And it was always predictable, before this trip. Get up, get kids to school, go to work, work, come home, help kids with school assignments, make dinner, go to bed. Over and over and over again."

"You really needed a change, didn't you."

Her mother's statement was spot on. "And I've really appreciated it." She leaned back, propping herself up with one hand. "If nothing else, Lincoln *is* a great kisser."

"I could have gone the rest of my existence not knowing that, dear."

Cheryl chuckled. "His lips make my body practically melt. Like butter on warm toast. When his arms are around me, he's literally the only thing I can focus on."

"I'm hanging up now. Love you."

"And the way he tastes is—"

The call went dead. Cheryl laughed out loud. Her mom was so great. She sent her a text telling her thanks for calling and that she loved her.

Love you too. Don't overthink things.

Her mom knew her too well. "Always overthink" was Cheryl's motto, her life mantra. Could she possibly turn that part of her off? She didn't think so.

CHERYL WOKE up excited and eager for the day, but as she got ready, her thoughts returned to her feelings the night before. Her hesitations. Had she ruined her evening with Lincoln by bringing up her doubts? She hoped not—she'd had a blast, and Lincoln had reassured her of everything.

Or had he?

He'd said "Let's take things a day at a time." As she thought about it while showering, she realized his answer had been exactly what she'd worried about.

Taking things a day rather than a week or a month at a time said the vacation was where their relationship was at, and once they got home, things would be different. And maybe they'd "take things a day at a time" there too, but she hadn't yet had the courage to ask him about kids.

Cheryl also knew him better now than she did back in high school, and she knew he was a people pleaser. He said what he needed to say in that moment to maintain harmony. He was also a talker and said things he didn't fully believe—he needed to hear them out loud before knowing what he was thinking. So, him saying her kids weren't an issue—as she suspected he would—wouldn't reassure her. Not really. His actions were what she'd need to pay attention to, once they got home. How he acted around Xander and Jade. How he treated her when he saw her put on the role of Mom. If he distanced himself.

Cheryl yanked her brush through her hair as she blew it dry, frustrated she was thinking those thoughts at all. Why couldn't she just enjoy herself for the rest of the vacation? There were only two days left.

Just let it be, Cheryl.

By the time she was out of the bathroom, she knew

two things. First, she was going to ask him about kids. And second, she wasn't going to read too deeply into his answer. She'd put the question out there, let him talk about it, then see if he had anything different to say later in the day.

Lincoln was in the kitchen, eating a bowl of cereal. He looked up when she entered, and an apologetic expression crossed his face. "Sorry I didn't cook anything. I didn't sleep well, and the only thing I wanted when I got up was cereal."

He'd left out several Tupperwares of cereal for her to choose from. She grabbed a bowl of one of them and joined him. "It's okay. Even cereal is more than I eat some mornings."

He didn't seem to hear her. He was staring off into space, in his own world.

"What's on the agenda?" she asked, hoping to get him talking so she could bring up her concerns. Or at least sense things out around them.

He shrugged. "Nothing, really. I'd like to go to the beach again. Maybe do some snorkeling."

"That would be fun." She paused. "Can I come?"

There. *That* got his attention. He looked up at her, his eyes wide. "Of course. The rest of my vacation is for you."

"How much longer do you have?"

"I'm flying home tomorrow."

"That soon?" Dismay filled Cheryl's chest. She was leaving the day after. She hadn't realized they'd also be going home on separate days.

He took her hand and gave it a squeeze. "When are *you* returning?"

"The day after tomorrow."

"It's only a day—it'll be fine."

She nodded but had her doubts. Now that he was talking, though, she wanted to ask her question. She chewed her lip, unable to eat while her stomach was filled with nervous anticipation. She didn't think she could outright ask how he'd feel about marrying a divorcee with two teenagers. That was way too close to home, and she doubted he'd be fully honest in his answer. Not that he'd lie, but again, he was a people pleaser. He'd reassure her that it would be fine, but then he'd drift away.

Or maybe he wouldn't. Maybe she was just assuming he'd break her heart again.

Still, she couldn't outright ask. It required far too much courage.

"Did you want kids growing up?"

There. That was innocent enough.

"Definitely. I wanted a big family—at least four kids, but preferably five. Five is a good number."

"And you pretty much raised your younger sisters, so you know how much work they are."

He shrugged. "My sisters were easy and not that much younger than me. I lucked out—both of them are hard workers and naturally obedient. Now, if *Joshua* had been younger, being 'Dad' would have been impossible."

"Was he rebellious?"

"Oooooh, yeah."

"And you don't handle that well."

He shrugged. "I don't have a lot of experience with it. But honestly, I don't think *anyone* handles it well."

Xander could get pretty rebellious when he wanted to, but Lincoln's answer was hardly incriminating. What else could she ask to figure out his feelings?

"If you had to pick a favorite age for a child, what would you go with?"

"Toddler," he said without hesitation. "Or just after that—when they're saying funny things and don't realize just how hilarious they are."

"That's my favorite age too," Cheryl said. Xander had given her a lot of grief once he'd hit ten years of age. Jade had been fine, and she was getting a lot more fun to talk to as she was aging, but there was something about toddlers that really tickled Cheryl.

She gave up on the conversation. As she thought about it, she realized she didn't want to ask her real question for valid reasons. First, it really *was* too blunt for only having been dating for a couple of days. And second, did she want to do that to herself this early?

No. No, she didn't.

She resolved yet again to enjoy their last day together, but his mood seemed affected too, and they didn't exchange many words while cleaning up from breakfast and heading out to the beach best known for snorkeling in the area.

Lincoln seemed a little happier later, when they left the water, and he held her hand as they walked back to their things on the beach, but he still wasn't in the mood to talk. That was fine—neither was she. They went back home and had sandwiches for lunch, then Lincoln invited Cheryl to relax on the couch with him. Cheryl braced herself for potentially tough conversations, but that didn't happen. They'd only been on the couch for a few minutes when someone knocked on the door.

Cheryl got up to get it and was surprised to see Chloe —the girl whose grandmother had had a panic attack—on the other side.

"Is your grandma okay?" Cheryl asked.

"Oh, she's much better. Thank you so much for your help. You guys came at the perfect time. I don't know what would have happened if you hadn't been there—she started calming down only when you arrived."

Cheryl's heart warmed. "I'm so glad we were able to help. What can we do for you?"

She felt—and heard—Lincoln approach. He put a hand on her shoulder, standing behind her, and Cheryl's heart warmed even more. She loved the simple action that told her he was claiming her.

Chloe's eyes raised to Lincoln, and her cheeks pinked. "I'm actually here to see Dr. Lincoln."

"Oh?" he said.

Lincoln stepped around Cheryl, eager to be of assistance, and Cheryl groaned inwardly. Not this again. She'd had to deal with Chloe's flirting during that whole panic attack ordeal. Lincoln had apparently been oblivious to it, but there was no way he'd miss the girl's attempts for attention a second time around. Especially with the hints Cheryl had left on their walk back home.

"I hurt my shoulder while helping my grandma, and it's still bothering me a lot. I was wondering if you'd take a look at it?"

He nodded and invited her in. Cheryl hovered in the background, not sure what to do.

Lincoln instructed Chloe to sit on the couch, then he started moving her arm around, checking its range of motion and watching her face for pain.

"Right there," she said, wincing.

Lincoln settled in next to her and began massaging the muscles, tendons, and ligaments. "Let me know when it hurts," he said.

Her eyes were closed. "It feels pretty good, actually."

Cheryl rolled her eyes. Defensiveness and possessiveness got a grip on her stomach, and she also sat down. "Tell us about yourself, Chloe," she said, hoping to distract both of them from the massage.

"I'm nearly finished at Hilo University," she said. "Only a few months to go."

Lincoln paused. "You're in *college*?"

She opened her eyes and looked at him. "Yes. What did you think—that I was older?"

"No. Younger. *Much* younger. As in, early high school and possibly even late junior high."

No wonder he hadn't caught her flirting. She was still too young, but nearly graduated from college wasn't completely outside the realm of possible for a man his age.

"Oh, man, I've always been told I have a baby face." She sent him a pouty expression. "Knowing I'm older doesn't make you dislike me, does it?"

Holy cow, that was forward.

"Of course not," Lincoln said.

Cheryl's jaw dropped. Was he actually going along with this? In front of Cheryl? There was no way—he had to be overly involved in the help he was giving Chloe.

But Cheryl nearly buried her face in her hands. The man was giving a massage to an attractive girl he just found out was actually a woman and not the jailbait he'd originally thought. Of *course* he'd be okay with the situation.

The more he talked, though, the more Cheryl realized he was in clinical, professional mode, not "find new girlfriend" mode. Chloe didn't seem to realize that. Or maybe she did, but didn't see it as a problem. Maybe she really *was* injured. Cheryl knew better than to assume that was the only reason she'd come to see Lincoln, though.

"What is your degree in?" she asked, wanting to control the conversation as much as possible. She knew it was petty, but her relationship with Lincoln was still too new for her to feel anything but insecure about this visit.

"Political science."

That was a surprise. "You're interested in politics?" Cheryl asked.

Chloe nodded, wincing as Lincoln worked over a sensitive area. "It's been a passion of mine for the last few years."

"My brother just resigned as a senator for Idaho."

Chloe's eyes fled to Cheryl's. "Really? Your brother is *Jack Davis*? Dang! He's so hot. Is he still single?"

Cheryl chuckled. He'd been one of only a few single senators—Chloe would obviously have noticed. "He's engaged to a friend of mine, actually, so no."

Chloe scoffed. "If there ain't no ring on his finger, he's still single."

Lincoln scowled at her, but didn't say anything, and Cheryl inwardly pumped her fist. Score for the old lady.

"They're pretty serious," she said. "I haven't seen anyone that much in love in a long time."

"Oh, well, I don't want to break that up." Chloe's gaze returned to Dr. Lincoln. "Not when there are other options around."

Whoa—outright flirting again. This girl was *bold*! How was Lincoln not noticing? But Chloe had been nearly this brazen while they helped her grandma, and he hadn't noticed then either. Maybe he wrote her off at that time because of her age. That wouldn't keep him back now, though.

Lincoln did a few more range of motion exercises with Chloe then said, "It's not too bad, but I'd still see if you can get a few appointments with a local physical therapist. The worst thing that could happen is reinjuring it while the muscles are inflamed—that could lead to tears or even a frozen shoulder."

Chloe's gaze didn't leave his face. "Can't I keep working with you?"

He shook his head. "I'm leaving tomorrow."

"That's sad." She hesitated. "I could come see you in Utah."

"I'd be fine with that if you're in the area, but that would be one heck of a bill to pay just for physical therapy."

"Money isn't an issue."

He got to his feet. "Well, that's good to know."

Why was that good to know? Was that an automatic, polite answer, or did he really like knowing Chloe had money? Cheryl was driving herself nuts not knowing the answers to her questions.

Chloe put a hand on his arm. "Thank you so much. I really appreciate it. How about I come back again this evening and have you do some work on me then too?"

Lincoln didn't skip a beat. Either he was being purposefully obtuse or he really didn't notice she was flirting. "You're going to want to rest it as much as possible today and the next couple of days. Don't use it unless you have to, and if it hurts, stop whatever you're doing immediately. I'd also suggest you take some ibuprofen or another inflammation reducer just in case."

Chloe trailed a hand up his arm to his perfectly formed bicep, obviously knowing he hadn't caught her flirting. "We could talk more over dinner—have you show me some exercises I could do at home."

Lincoln took her injured arm and said, "Here, I'll show you them now."

Cheryl would have grinned at the expression of frustration on Chloe's face if it weren't for her current mood. The girl was desperate for attention.

Lincoln didn't seem to notice Chloe's less-than-excited response to the exercises. Small victory, but it still made Cheryl feel a little better.

By the time Chloe left, she had handed Lincoln a piece of paper with her number on it, kissed him on the cheek, and given him a lingering hug.

"In case you weren't aware, she's into you," Cheryl said after the door was shut.

"I know."

Cheryl paused. "You actually noticed?"

"She kissed the corner of my mouth. It's hard to miss something like that."

"If you realized what she was doing, why didn't you stop her?"

Lincoln gazed steadily at Cheryl. "Are you jealous?"

She hesitated, not sure how to answer. Or how he *wanted* her to answer. "She's young, apparently she's loaded, and she's into you. If the roles were reversed, how would you feel?"

"It depends on if you're into younger men or not." He said it with a smile, but Cheryl wouldn't relent. She held his gaze, waiting for a serious answer.

"You're being a little petty about this."

"I just want to know if my—if you see a future with her." That had been close. She'd almost said boyfriend. They were *not* boyfriend and girlfriend—he'd never said

ANDREA KATE PEARSON

they were, and she for sure hadn't. She'd remember if that conversation had taken place.

He shrugged. "No. I've enjoyed spending time with you. You'll always be the highlight of this trip."

But? What was he getting at? Was he holding her at arm's distance on purpose? "We're still taking things a day at a time?"

"It's all I have to give." He pulled her into a hug, then placed a kiss on her forehead. "Especially now. I don't handle jealousy well. Your disdain for Chloe was rolling off of you in waves larger than anything we've seen at the ocean so far." He rubbed his eyes and sighed. "Cheryl, I see hundreds of attractive women a year. If not patients, their daughters or sisters or aunts or even the occasional single mom. If you can't handle me working with someone beautiful, well . . . I don't know what to say."

He was right, but still, he'd said nothing that helped her feel better. The fact that he was dismissive of her feelings left her hollow inside. She'd known all along that she was acting insecure and immature, both very unattractive traits. But he'd done nothing to reassure her that his feelings went as deep as hers, that he was there for the long-haul. Instead, he'd accused her of being petty.

Ugh.

Cheryl started cleaning the kitchen in earnest, needing something to put her mind to. Lincoln retreated to his room, and she breathed a sigh of relief, glad to have some alone time.

$\mathcal{L}$incoln berated himself for a solid hour for not reassuring Cheryl that he was hers. The truth was he wasn't sure if he *was* hers. He knew she'd been hurt a lot in the past, and even by him. But was she able to move on? From everything he'd seen so far, she wasn't—she held grudges, got offended easily, and mistrusted.

Dinner was quiet, and he knew she had a lot on her mind. He did too. He wanted to talk about everything—to get them on the same page—but he wasn't sure how. Every time they'd had a conversation lately, it seemed as if the wrong things came out of his mouth and he ended up hurting her yet again. But he wasn't the only one doing the hurting. It still stung that she'd so quickly assumed he'd drop her for some ditzy blonde bombshell. He wasn't even into blondes, and he most certainly wasn't into women who were that forward.

And yet, Cheryl had decided before even talking to him about it that he'd enjoyed the attention and had milked it instead of recognizing just how uncomfortable he'd been with Chloe's hands and eyes on him.

Besides, Chloe had faked the injury. He hadn't wanted to embarrass her by accusing her of it, but the areas that were "tender" had migrated so frequently while he'd been massaging that he couldn't keep up with them. She obviously couldn't either. Plus, as she'd driven away, she'd reached into the backseat of her car to grab something. An action like that would have been exceptionally painful if not impossible for the injury she'd pretended to have.

He wondered if he had pointed that out to Cheryl, if she would have felt better about the situation. He didn't know.

And one other thing that was bothering him. He knew she had other concerns—deeper ones she wasn't sharing. The fact that she was withholding them from him so that he couldn't help her feel better about them really frustrated him.

Still, he felt as if it was all his fault, that if he had made the Chloe thing better, Cheryl would have gotten over it. He hated it when someone he cared for was annoyed with him.

Lincoln breathed a sigh of relief as he realized he *did* care for Cheryl. That none of the emotions and kisses they'd shared had been fake.

But how to make it right?

After they were done eating, he pulled her into his arms. "I'm sorry," he whispered.

"For what?" she asked, not looking up at him.

"I don't know—I feel like you're withdrawing because of me. I don't know how to say what I'm thinking, and I don't know how to help you feel better. Words come out of my mouth that I don't mean, and it's not until they're out that I recognize they're not really how I feel."

"My mom is the same way," she said.

His relief was tangible, but brief. "Why are you still pulling away, then?"

She looked up at him. "I don't want to get hurt again."

A flash of frustration hit him, and before he could—yet again—think through his words, they spilled out. "And you don't think I'm not worried about getting hurt, Cheryl? You don't think I'm nervous about rejection? You heard my stories. You know how hard it is for me to open up. Didn't I say we needed to take things a day at a time? That wasn't just for *us*, it was for *me* too. You're pushing us further than we need to go—than we're ready. Are you *wanting* me to break up with you? Because it feels like that's what you're pushing us toward."

"You can't break up with someone you're not dating."

That was a slap to the face. "What do you mean? I don't kiss girls I'm not dating."

"You could have told me that."

"Are you serious? Are we really arguing over a stupid DTR?"

"I have no idea what that means, but this is not something 'stupid' to discuss."

"Define the Relationship—a conversation immature people have to have when they're insecure in a relationship."

Cheryl stepped away from him, folded her arms, and glared. "Why do you have to put little insults into our conversations?"

He blinked. "What are you talking about?" Then it dawned on him. Oh, man. Again with saying things he didn't mean. "Cheryl, I wasn't calling *you* immature or insecure."

"Yes, you were. I needed to know we're in a relationship. You said that needing that conversation equals being insecure."

He closed his eyes and rubbed them. "You're right, and I'm sorry about that. It wasn't what I meant, though. I told you—words come out of my mouth before I know what I'm thinking and feeling."

She tightened her arms around herself. "Then what *are* you feeling? What do *you* want, Lincoln? Do you want an old, divorcee with kids or a cute, college girl who's loaded?"

He shook his head. "How are we even having this conversation?"

"Just answer the question."

"Why is it so important to you?"

"Because you haven't said anything to tell me I'm safe to give you my heart. You've kissed me and held me close, but Lincoln, *anyone* can do that with an attractive member of the opposite sex. You didn't come to Hawaii to be with me, and spending time with me was a given since we're stuck in the same place. None of this encourages me that you won't turn around and break my heart."

She was right. She was totally right. And he had no idea how to respond.

She obviously sensed he didn't have an answer because she said, "Let's just talk in the morning."

Despite the fact that he knew she was right, and he knew what his answer should have been, he still couldn't give it to her. He wasn't sure he wanted to. She'd started distancing herself before he'd had a chance to prove himself, and he did *not* want to feel like he was begging her to date him.

At least he hadn't wasted years before finding out "they" would never work out.

❧

LINCOLN TOSSED and turned for several hours, inspecting their conversation from every angle. Could he have handled things better? Most definitely. Could he make things better? He wasn't sure about that.

Because his earlier thoughts were true. *Cheryl* had hesitated first. She'd pulled away before he could have understood what her concerns were. And as he thought back to their time together, he saw that he'd been reassuring her all along. From his willingness to leave when he was obviously not wanted, and then later, by building her up when he could tell she was insecure about her current landing point in life.

And yet, she'd still been the first to put up shields, demanding he reassure her verbally. But where would it end? Would he constantly have to *tell* her she was the only one he wanted?

Would she ever get to a point where she trusted his words *and* his actions? Would she constantly question everything he did and said?

If she never trusted him, where would that leave him?

Lincoln rolled to a sitting position, thinking over his decision before acting on it. He was going to go for a drive. He wasn't sleeping anyway. Might as well get out and do something. He'd head up to Mauna Kea to see the stars. That was what he'd planned to do with Cheryl before she'd gotten weird.

And so, at two in the morning, he packed his bags and put them in the car, knowing he wouldn't have time to come back before he needed to be at the airport. He cleaned up his room, then sent a reminder on his phone to text Cheryl later. Ha. Like he'd forget. He put his things in the car, looked up the mountain on his maps application, then pulled out of the driveway and followed the directions.

As he drove, he was surprised to find himself mentally saying goodbye to Cheryl. The vacation had been the largest emotional roller coaster he'd ever been on, and he would always look back at certain parts of it with fondness. He'd look back at other parts with trepidation, frustration, and definitely regret, though.

He gripped his steering wheel, staring out at the darkness in front of his car as he drove, reminding himself that Cheryl had started pulling away first.

Even if he *wasn't* saying goodbye and even if he *wanted* to spend the rest of his life with her, he couldn't force her to accept him, to be okay with what he did for a living. To be comfortable with him being around other women, even attractive ones.

He couldn't force her to be what he needed and wanted.

That realization made his stomach ache. Had he been trying to put his idea of what a woman should be on her? He didn't think so—he felt like he'd been fair and open with her about pretty much everything. But would he have regrets? Probably. He always did.

It took him over an hour to get to the Onizuka Center on Mauna Kea. The parking lot was empty, as he'd expected it to be, and he stopped in the middle of it, pulling the top down on his convertible and gazing up at the stars, absolutely amazed at how bright they were.

"Why am I still single?" he asked, relishing in the complete darkness and aloneness. A good out-loud conversation with himself was exactly what he needed. "Is it really because marriage isn't for me? Or is there another reason? And what was the point of this vacation? Why did I have to get to know Cheryl, to like her—even love her— if I'm not supposed to get married?"

He shook his head, hating that the backs of his eyes were starting to burn. He was *not* going to cry. "Why *can't* I get married? Why can't I have the joy that so many other people seem to experience? Why does such a simple part of life always evade me and seem just out of my grasp?"

Sure, he was happy—he loved his job, and he loved the people he worked with. But he felt like he'd been at a standstill for years. Neither moving up nor down. Not growing. Incapable of reaching the next step on his own. He hated that feeling. Like he was stunted because of some greater power that was keeping him from the growth that marriage would bring.

He knew without that bond, his growth really *was* stunted. He knew he wasn't who he was supposed to be, that a part of him was missing.

He'd come to accept that there'd always be a hole in his heart and life. But what if it really wasn't meant to be that way? What if his emotions—and the fear of pain— were the things holding him back from finding true love?

And what if he'd always searched in the wrong places for that happiness?

For the first time in his life, he forced himself to look back on the past two decades of dating. It was hard—very hard—but he felt like it was important. Necessary, even.

Brittany had been a relationship of convenience. He saw that now. She'd always been there—calming his fears, comforting his pain. She'd helped him through a huge, pivotal moment in his life, and he'd thought she'd *always* be there. But she was right—they, not just her, weren't in love enough. He'd been attracted to her, enjoyed spending time with her, but he hadn't been *happy* with her.

His next girlfriend—the one who'd been pursuing her career—hadn't ever fully opened up to him. And now he realized he'd never opened up to her either. How could he, when she didn't trust him? She'd also been selfish to the core. Not once had she ever done something for him. Everything had always been about herself.

And then there was Taylor, the girl who hated Utah's mountains. She'd loved him, but obviously not enough to settle down where it was the most logical for them to settle. She'd been disappointed he hadn't chased her out to Kansas, but she'd at least understood the financial reasons.

He had no desire to leave Utah. Not only was he committed to staying financially, but he'd come to love the people and the mountains and neighborhoods and even the little hometown grocery store he shopped at. Alpine was a unique city, full of very wealthy, but also very friendly people. That wasn't a combination that came together often. Maybe Taylor felt the same way about Kansas. And if they both loved "home" more than each other, well . . . that said a lot.

Cheryl didn't seem to want to leave Utah. Her brother had just returned and was settling in, getting married. Her kids were in school there. Her mom had retired there. She'd not once mentioned the desire to move. And she loved the mountains too.

Not only that, but he couldn't forget the happiness

he'd felt with her. The rightness of having her by him, in his arms, and the joy he'd had in most of their conversations. How easy it had been to discuss his past with her. And no, he hadn't ever told her that he'd come to believe he wasn't meant to get married, but all of their other conversations had been deep and heartfelt.

Compared to his ex-girlfriends, she seemed so perfect for him. So why had she pulled away first? And after only a day or two of dating?

That was what hurt the most. She hadn't even given him a chance to prove himself—to prove he would love her forever—before she'd started backing away.

None of his previous rejections had been this unfair, this harsh. None of them had left him feeling so strongly like he needed to prove himself to someone.

He couldn't make her choose to trust him. Yes, maybe he should have reassured her earlier. But the outcome wouldn't have changed what he was now realizing. Cheryl needed to move at her own pace, not his, and if that meant moving away from him, he had to accept that.

Lincoln stayed up on the mountain for several more hours, thinking through his thoughts, dozing a bit, and then watching the sunrise. By the time he was ready to head back down, he was due at the airport.

And he still hadn't come to peace where Cheryl was concerned. Despite his practical side telling him he was doing the right thing by allowing her to step back, his heart hurt more than he'd thought possible.

Either way, a few days of separation was a good idea.

CHAPTER 17

The house was quiet when Cheryl woke up, and she brushed her teeth and got ready for the day, keeping an ear toward the doors, waiting to hear Lincoln stir in his room or come through the front door. She still stung from their conversation the night before. She couldn't believe the things he'd said and insinuated. She wasn't immature or petty or pathetic or anything like that.

At least, she didn't believe so. Sure, she'd overreacted about Chloe . . . but thinking back, it still seemed warranted. Lincoln hadn't done anything unprofessional, but he'd done nothing to validate her feelings. And maybe he didn't need to—maybe she was expecting something that wouldn't happen in *any* relationship.

Man, she was ready to have a break from her thoughts. It was time for a conversation.

She knocked on Lincoln's door. No one answered, and she opened it, stepping inside. It was empty, his bed stripped and suitcase gone. Had he left for the airport without saying goodbye?

Pain hit her hard in the chest, and she gasped at the

shock from it, tears building in her eyes. They'd definitely not seen eye-to-eye the night before, but did that warrant deserting her? No, it absolutely did not. If he couldn't handle one little fight, what would he do if and when things got really difficult?

Her jaw hardened, and she felt another wall building around her heart.

Good riddance. She didn't need a goodbye from him. She didn't need another conversation with him at all, for that matter.

Cheryl scowled, returning to her room and grabbing her phone, planning on heading to the beach where she could work through her disappointment, anger, and frustration.

She woke her phone up, surprised to see a text from Lincoln, sent earlier that morning.

Heading to the airport now. Sorry I didn't say goodbye in person, but I felt it would be better this way. We both need some time to cool down and figure out what we want from life. Our priorities, basically. Thank you for a great vacation. Give your mom my thanks too.

Cheryl's scowl deepened as her finger flew across her phone screen.

Tell her yourself, you jerk. And while you're at it, I hope you do figure out your priorities.

Changing her mind about sending such hateful words, she deleted the text, then put her phone away. She knew what she needed, and it definitely wasn't someone telling her to decide what she wanted from life. Not at her age, thank you very much.

She needed a man who was man enough not to put someone down for being insecure. A man who loved her for who she was, kids, baggage, and all. A man who accepted her *with* her weaknesses and didn't expect her to change.

Apparently, that wasn't Lincoln.

She jammed her phone into her back pocket, then slammed the door behind her, needing to blow off some of the steam and anger building. She stormed down the steps to the driveway, anger making her legs pump quickly and her breath come in short gasps.

She couldn't believe his words. Figure out what they wanted from life? *She* knew what she wanted. *He* obviously didn't.

At least she'd finally have the opportunity to move on. She'd had the chance to kiss the one man she'd dreamed most of kissing, of being alone with him, hearing what made him tick, and now that that wish had been fulfilled, she was ready to get over him, to never see him again.

Grrr! He was so infuriating. Cheryl kicked a rock off the street, scowling at it. He thought it would be better not to say goodbye in person? Did he expect her to cry? To fall apart at his departure? She *wouldn't* have. He'd left no reason for her to get emotional—other than angry.

And back to the thing about giving her mom his thanks. Was he not planning on working with Helen anymore? Was he scared she'd make him do something he didn't want to do again? That she'd ask tough questions?

He'd *better* be scared. Cheryl's mom wouldn't have any problem putting him in his place.

Cheryl walked the trail near the beach, finding her way over and around the large volcanic rocks. The rough terrain suited her mood perfectly, and the aggressive waves gave her anger an outlet. She picked up rocks, throwing them into the frothing waves, watching them disappear into the deeper areas or get twisted and raked across the sand in the shallow spots.

She was better off without Lincoln. She didn't need him. She didn't need any man. She had her kids, and yes, life got lonely, but it was better than this anger that practically consumed her.

Her relationship with Lincoln had been very short. And they'd experienced the whole gamut of emotions. Anyone who was able to strike that many emotions in just a few days was someone she needed to avoid.

She hated feeling this way—so torn and conflicted and mad. Underneath it all, though, was pain. He'd practically betrayed her. At least, that's how it felt. Why hadn't he said goodbye in person? They could have resolved so many things with just one more conversation.

But even if they'd talked again, would she have been able to tell him what she was really concerned about? She'd had plenty of opportunity to bring up her kids and had hesitated each time.

After pacing the beach, stumbling over rocks when tears threatened to spill, she finally took a seat and watched the waves for a while before responding to Lincoln's text.

Hope you have a safe flight home.

It was the nicest thing she could think to say. "I mean," she whispered, "I don't actually want him to die . . ." But saying anything else felt dishonest. Even a simple "goodbye" wouldn't have been the truth. She felt anything but good about the bye they'd exchanged.

CHAPTER 18

*L*incoln stared at Cheryl's text for several moments, not fully computing the words. The exhaustion from not sleeping had finally caught up to him at the airport, and it was all he could do not to fall asleep even while standing. His flight didn't leave until 11:00am, and he was starting to regret turning in his rental car. The food at the airport was expensive and the selection not great. Of course, driving when that tired wasn't a good idea, so being stuck at the airport wasn't the worst thing that could happen to him.

He turned his attention back to his phone. She was upset—it would take an idiot not to realize that. No goodbye, no thank you, no nothing.

Did he deserve any of that, though? He wasn't sure. He had a sinking feeling he'd handled everything very poorly. But self-preservation instincts were so hard to go against.

He finally boarded the plane, practically a zombie. Unfortunately, his emotions were severely affected by the exhaustion, and he really struggled with the desire to call Cheryl and beg for forgiveness.

Lincoln knew one thing for sure, though—making any sort of decision while this emotional and this exhausted was a bad idea. He needed to get home, get back to his routine, get some sleep, and clear his mind.

After that, if he still wanted to call Cheryl and beg forgiveness, he'd do it.

Something told him that wouldn't happen, though. They were too incompatible, too different, too unyielding and unbending.

You can't force someone to love you.

Lincoln settled into his seat, grateful Helen had chosen one by a window. It meant he wouldn't be interrupted. He asked for a blanket, did up his seatbelt, then shoved the blanket between his head and the wall of the plane and fell asleep.

CHAPTER 19

*C*heryl spent the rest of the morning hanging out at the beach and watching the waves, wanting them to calm her but not feeling ready to release her negative emotions just yet. When she'd had her fill of the ocean, she headed back to the vacation rental. She was grateful to find Susan and Tom home. Instead of wallowing in her misery, she chatted with them, getting caught up on their kids and grandkids.

Underneath it all, her anger gradually dissipated, but its absence only allowed the hurt to swell up. If only she'd told Lincoln what her true fears were instead of expecting the worst from him.

If only she'd trusted him.

Ironic how she'd expected him to trust her, how she'd been mad when he hadn't. But he'd been hurt far more by life than she ever had. Her divorce had been emotionless and easy—they both wanted out. But Lincoln had had his heart broken multiple times, and even before that, he'd experienced some pretty awful things. So why had she expected him to be the first to go out on a limb?

How immature could someone get? He was right—she'd been petty.

And now that he was gone, a different part of her ached. A part of her heart that hadn't been touched in a long, long time.

Somehow, during their long conversations where he'd opened up completely to her, she'd fallen in love with him. And not the superficial love she'd felt during high school. This time, it was genuine, sincere, and honest. Lincoln was a good man, and she'd totally blown it.

That hurt more than anything. *She* was the one who'd ruined a potential future with him this time.

Not only that, but she'd basically rejected him by not opening up to him, not fully letting him in, even after he'd totally opened himself up to her. She'd done to him the thing he'd feared the most from a woman.

Could she make things right again? Did she want to? She wasn't sure. Her pride still stung from the things he'd said, despite knowing he was right about them. Knowing he was right made it more painful, actually.

But was she willing to let a perfectly good man slip through her fingers for a second time, especially when she held the power this time? She didn't know.

CHAPTER 20

*L*incoln slept fitfully the whole flight home. When he landed and turned his phone back on, he half expected to have received a text or something from Cheryl, but nothing was there. As other passengers deboarded, he stared at his phone, trying to understand what he needed and wanted.

He wanted to hear Cheryl's voice. But what did he *need*? Was it her? And what did *she* want?

Lincoln leaned back against his seat and stared at the console overhead, searching his feelings. Something told him to give her a call, that he still didn't have all the information. Especially the part he knew she was holding back from him.

As soon as he'd gotten off the plane and found a quiet area in the airport where he could have a private conversation, he called her.

Cheryl answered on the third ring, her voice quiet and hesitant.

He didn't even greet her, just went right into what was on his mind. "In all of our recent conversations—

arguments, if you will—I could tell you were holding something back and pulling away. Cheryl, I need to know if my intuition is correct. Without all the info, I can't possibly approach you the way you need to be approached. Is there something you're worrying about where we're concerned?"

She didn't respond right away. "I don't know, Lincoln."

He shook his head in frustration, grabbing the hair at the base of his neck with his free hand. "Yes, you *do*."

He expected her to get defensive, but she only sighed in response.

Lincoln waited again, but once more, she didn't say anything. "I know you hate confrontation. I also know that sharing your thoughts and feelings—especially the ones that make you vulnerable and exposed—is uncomfortable. It's hard for me too, as you've recently learned. But Cheryl, if you hold back any part of you in a relationship, the man you're with will eventually sense it, and he'll start to hold back part of himself too."

He gripped his phone, turning to face the wall. "You can't find true happiness without risking rejection."

His words hit him square in the chest. It was as if he'd been speaking to himself. But he wasn't ready to examine those words just yet. This conversation was about Cheryl, not him.

She signed again. "You're right. It's just . . . so close to my heart."

"I wanted to be close to your heart too." He still did.

She remained silent. Then all at once, in a rush, she said, "Yes, I've held something back. I've been thinking over all of your rejections, and I've begun to worry that those other women shared the same concern I now have

—that you don't really want kids. I know that's a huge assumption on my part, but every time I've mentioned my kids when I've been around you, your entire mood has shifted and you get this little frown on your face. And so, I don't think you can handle the idea of dating a woman who already has children.

"I had a lot of fun the last few days," she continued, "and I understand where you're coming from. Kids are hard. But they're also incredibly rewarding, if you give them a chance. Especially mine." She paused as if waiting for an answer, but Lincoln's brain had come to a complete halt. "So, no. I don't want to be with someone who can't accept me for who I am—kids and all—or give me reassurance when I need it. Goodbye, Lincoln."

And then she ended the call.

Lincoln didn't lower the phone for several seconds after she'd gone. He stared at the wall in front of him, then turned and sat in a chair in front of it. *Had* he shown displeasure when she'd mentioned her kids? He didn't remember thinking anything negative about them.

Lincoln rubbed his eyes, the exhaustion hitting him again. He'd never had a positive experience with kids, other than his sisters, but they were too close in age to him to count. He hadn't had a *negative* one with kids, either. He was as neutral as you could get. But somehow, in his attempt to show that neutrality, Cheryl had caught a slight hesitation where hers were concerned. He hadn't even been aware that hesitation existed.

His inexperience with children was what caused her to pause where their relationship was concerned. Kids had never entered the equation for him—he'd always wanted a family, but as he'd gotten older, he'd had to adjust to the idea that it might not happen for him.

Somehow, that adjusting had played out across his face while talking to Cheryl.

Realizing he needed to grab his suitcase before they hauled it off the baggage carousel, he got up and followed the signs to the luggage pickup area, lost in his thoughts, trying to process what he'd just learned.

Once he got in his car, he gave Helen a call, hooking his phone up to the car's Bluetooth system so he could drive while talking. He wouldn't be able to fully understand his thoughts unless he talked through them.

"Cheryl thinks I don't like her kids," he said as soon as Helen answered. "It took a while, but I finally got that out of her just now, over the phone."

"Hello, Lincoln," Helen said, a smile in her voice. "It's nice to talk to you too."

"I don't understand how she got that impression," he said, ignoring her joke. "I don't have enough experience with kids to know if I like them or not. I'm completely neutral on the topic."

"Cheryl would pick up on that and view it as you being against them. She's very sensitive where her kids are concerned and sometimes sees things that aren't there."

Lincoln nodded. "Like me frowning when she mentioned them. I don't even remember having any emotions at all when she brought them up!"

"Now that I've got you on the phone," Helen said, "what are your intentions with my daughter?"

Talk about a loaded question. Especially after his recent arguments with Cheryl. Lincoln dropped his head back against the headrest. "I honestly don't know. Hawaii was a lot of fun, and I felt like something was there, but Cheryl's walls . . . there are so many of them." He had a lot of them too, he had to admit. It wasn't just her who'd done the pushing away.

"She's like an onion. You have to peel back the layers one at a time, even if it makes you cry."

"That's a pleasant thought."

Helen chuckled. "Do you like her?"

"Yes. I do." That was an easy answer.

"Enough to see where things might go? Enough to be with her, in a long-term relationship?"

That, he wasn't sure. "I don't know, Helen. I've been rejected so many times."

"I know you have—your life has been one heartache after another."

He was grateful he'd told her about his parents' accident and the various rejections he'd experienced. Helen was the sort of person a talker like him had zero problem opening up to.

"Were you happy with Cheryl?"

"Of course—she's easy to be with."

"I don't mean that. I mean, did she fill your heart with joy? Did being around her make you feel complete?"

He had to think that one over. Only a couple of days of dating weren't a lot to go off of. But as he thought about Cheryl—her smiles, her selflessness, the hesitant way she'd shared her story with him . . . his heart filled with warmth and happiness. As he looked beyond the recent hurt and pain, back to when negative emotions hadn't entered the picture, he realized a part of him had clicked that hadn't ever before.

If she came around and trusted him—if she opened up to him all the way—he had no reason not to pursue a relationship with Cheryl.

Nothing else about her threw up flags. And maybe

he'd put too much emphasis on her pulling away first. Maybe he'd started looking for a reason to end things with her before he could get hurt—before she had a chance to fully say no to him, or even yes.

Something his mom had told him a year before her accident came back. She'd said that you sometimes have to date a lot of wrong people before you're ready for your right person. That those wrong people help shape you, help you understand who you are and what you want, that they help prepare you for the person most likely to make you happy.

Lincoln sighed. It had felt like his girlfriends had all torn chunks of his heart away, but maybe those parts were really rough edges that had needed to be smoothed down, to help him be more compassionate, more patient, more able to understand the pain other people experienced.

Maybe they'd helped prepare him for Cheryl.

"I'm glad you're giving my question a good amount of thought."

"I am." He changed lanes on the freeway, heading toward Alpine, still musing over Helen's questions.

Cheryl had brought him joy. It was a different happiness than his previous girlfriends had brought. It was deeper, calmer, more mature. He hadn't noticed it as much. The youthful energy hadn't been there, and its absence made him feel like things weren't right. But he'd changed over the years. He wasn't young anymore, so expecting that zest was unrealistic.

Besides, all of his heartache had tempered him.

"Let me pose a different question to you," Helen said. "How would you feel if you never saw Cheryl again? Or if —God forbid—she passed away on her way home from Hawaii?"

"That's a horrible thought for a mother to have!"

"Of course it is. Answer the question."

Pain blossomed in Lincoln's chest as he thought of the possibility of never hearing Cheryl's laughter again. Of never looking into her eyes, sensing the depth and wisdom there. Of never hearing that wisdom come out her mouth in a deep conversation. Of never seeing her smile again.

The pain spread through his whole body when he thought about how he'd feel if she stopped existing. It was so strong, it made him gasp for breath. His heart pounded against his ribcage, making him feel like a cornered animal wanting to fight for survival. For Cheryl's survival.

For the survival of their relationship.

"I can't imagine that—I would do anything in my power to protect her, to keep her safe."

"And do you like kissing her? Because attraction is a huge part of all of this, and if you're not attracted to her, you—"

"Attraction isn't a problem." Staying in the same house with Cheryl had kept him up at night, for crying out loud. It had been hard not to think only of his attraction to her.

"Then you have your answer."

For a moment, Lincoln doubted Helen. Of course she'd say that—she was Cheryl's mother. But *was* it his answer? How would he feel if he saw Cheryl right then, with a big smile on her face? If he took her into his arms and apologized for everything he'd said, for not reassuring her, for not letting her know that he was all hers?

The thought filled his heart with warmth. It eased out the pain, pushed back the ache and sadness.

He *wanted* to be with Cheryl. He wanted *Cheryl*.

"Helen, she started pulling away first," he said. "I can't force her to want to be with me."

Helen sighed. "She's very sensitive where her kids are concerned. That will always be a sore spot for her. But if you convince her that her kids are the best things ever—which they are, by the way—you'll have her so wrapped around your finger she'll never want to leave your side."

Was that true? "But are her kids the only thing that caused her to hesitate where I'm concerned?"

"Cheryl isn't a very complex person," Helen said. "She has deep thoughts, but her needs are simple. Love her, and love her kids. Then don't worry about anything else—it'll fall into place as it should."

Lincoln thought that over. Could it really be that simple? Getting along with other people came naturally to him. And teenagers are people too.

"What do I do?" he said.

"That's between you and Cheryl's kids. It's time we arrange something. They've been dying to meet you."

"Perfect. Should I head straight to your room?"

Helen chuckled. "Lincoln. It's eleven at night."

Lincoln blinked. How had he not even noticed the time? He'd barely even been aware it was dark, for crying out loud.

If that wasn't evidence of his love for Cheryl, he didn't know what was.

Love . . . he was in *love* with her.

A grin split his face. Yes, he was. He really was.

"Okay, tomorrow morning, then." He bit his lip. "Oh, and sorry for calling so late."

"Don't worry about it—I haven't been sleeping much anyway."

"I'm sorry to hear that."

"It's part of getting older, dear. You'll be here soon enough—enjoy your restful nights while you have them."

They exchanged goodbyes, and Lincoln ended the call.

He couldn't wait to meet Cheryl's kids. He also couldn't wait to get to bed. His body was so confused. The jet lag would be rough this time around. Luckily, he was exhausted and hadn't slept well on the plane. Sleep should come easily.

The rest of the drive went quickly enough, and soon, Lincoln was in his own bed. And sleep did come quickly as thoughts of Cheryl flitted through his mind.

He loved her, and he was going to tell her.

CHAPTER 21

𝒞heryl's flight landed in Salt Lake City at four in the afternoon. She was exhausted from getting to the airport at two am, and Dr Pepper had been the only thing that kept her awake and alert during her drive back to Alpine. She'd tried to watch movies on the plane, but none of the action flicks appealed to her, and romance was the last thing she wanted. She ended up watching kids' movies. Instead of paying attention to the plots, though, she hadn't been able to stop thinking about Lincoln, and her questions accompanied her during her drive home too.

What had he thought about her revelation about children? She knew he had a thing against them, and his hesitation on the phone had cemented it in. A small part of her celebrated that her doubts had been proven correct, that she'd saved herself from getting stood up by him again. Metaphorically speaking, this time.

"And he *would* have rejected you. You *know* he would have," she whispered to herself as she drove.

But if she'd scored a victory, why did she feel so hollow

185

inside? Why did it feel like she'd come out as the loser? Why did it feel like she'd moved away from something that could have made her happier than she'd ever been?

"You don't need a man to be happy, Cheryl."

Her kids should be enough.

And yet, they weren't.

That made Cheryl even sadder. They'd been her whole life for so long, and thinking that they weren't enough made her feel like she'd betrayed them somehow.

Why, though? Why couldn't she have them *and* Lincoln?

Was that even possible? Did it even matter? If he wasn't interested in her *and* her kids, she wouldn't have the option to choose him.

Her thoughts circled around and around to all of these arguments so much where she was going mad. Instead of driving straight home, she went to see Kara.

Kara squealed when she opened the door, throwing herself in Cheryl's arms. "How was Hawaii?"

"Crazy, actually. I'm sorry I didn't call or text while I was there."

Kara waved her off. "I didn't expect you to—I knew you needed to be alone in your head for a while."

Cheryl leveled a glare at Kara. "*Alone?* You mean, alone with *Lincoln Tanner?*"

An innocent expression crossed Kara's face. "What do you mean? Was *he* there? What are the odds of that happening . . ." Her voice faded off, and a slight grin tickled the corners of her mouth.

"You can't pretend not to have been a part of all that finagling, Kara. I can see right through your false innocence."

Kara plopped down on the couch in her living room,

patting the seat next to her. "Fine. I admit, your mom, Lincoln's assistant, his brother, and I were up to our elbows planning your life." Her grin faded, and she turned to Cheryl. "Did it work? How did it go?"

Cheryl groaned, dropping her head back against the couch. "I don't know, Kara."

"Is he a good kisser?"

Cheryl whipped her head up, staring at Kara, her eyes wide. "How did you know? Did my mom tell you?"

Kara jumped to her feet, laughing and shouting, "I *knew* it! I *knew* you'd end up kissing! And no, your mom didn't say a thing."

"I'm surprised. She told Xander and Jade."

"I haven't seen them all week—Jack took them camping."

Cheryl blinked. "Whoa. That was brave of him. Not even I have done that, and I'm their mom."

"Yeah, he said it was about time."

Cheryl laughed. "*He* said that? My stuffy, uptight younger brother?"

"I know, crazy, right? He's really relaxed since coming home."

"It's because of you."

Kara's cheeks reddened, and a quiet smile appeared on her face. "I know. He's so wonderful." She blinked, her gaze returning to Cheryl. "Enough about Jack. Details. I need details right this moment or I might explode."

Cheryl chuckled. "Fine. But you might not be happy with how I handled things."

"Why wouldn't I?" Kara held her palm toward Cheryl. "Wait. Don't tell me that part yet. Let's start at the beginning."

So Cheryl told Kara about her trip to Hawaii. How

the earthquake collapsed the road and forced her and Lincoln to be in the same house, how Susan and Tom's return put them in the same apartment—that made Kara squeal with excitement—and how they'd spent time together helping people. How that had made Cheryl fall in love with Lincoln all over again.

And Cheryl realized now for sure that that was what had happened. Lincoln was the most amazing man she'd ever been around. He was selfless and enthusiastic and energetic, and being near him didn't deplete her energy stores as it usually did with people like that. His personality breathed life back into her. It made her feel things she hadn't felt in years. It made her tingle, just thinking about it now.

Cheryl then told Kara about their first kiss, and kissing on the black-sand beach and kissing at the volcano, and kissing after getting back from that day trip . . . It had been so much fun.

"Wow. You've really got it bad! So, are you guys official now? Can we start doubling?"

Tears burned the backs of Cheryl's eyes. "Not exactly." She dropped her face to her hands. "I think I royally screwed up."

"That would explain your mood when you arrived. I figured something was off if you didn't bounce your way inside."

"I don't bounce my way anywhere."

Kara smiled. "What happened, then? Did you overthink the relationship?"

Cheryl peeked at Kara through her fingers. "How did you know?"

"Because you overthink everything."

"I know. It's a real problem."

"Sometimes. And sometimes it's a good thing."

"Not this time. I freaked out when he didn't tell me how he felt when I wanted or thought I needed him to." She dropped her hands. "He's had his heart broken several times. And here, I expected him to go out on a limb without me giving him any sort of encouragement."

"Kissing is encouragement."

"Yeah, that's physical, though. He's a talker—he needed me to *tell* him how I felt. And I didn't. I also didn't tell him the doubts I had, so he had no way to talk to me about them."

"What doubts?"

"My kids. He'd get this little frown every time I mentioned them."

"Like he didn't want you to bring them up or something?"

Cheryl nodded. "Just like that."

"Do you think you could have read too much into it? Maybe he wasn't frowning about them. Maybe he was frowning because he wanted to know more about them—understand how you felt about them. You say he likes and needs conversation. He probably expected you to talk about them with him. And you didn't, did you?"

Cheryl shook her head. "I was too nervous he'd reject me over them."

Kara made a good point. If Lincoln needed verbal reassurance for anything in his life, he'd need it about everything. And he'd probably waited for her to bring up the topic. And when she hadn't, he'd withdrawn.

As she'd suspected, she'd forced him to reject her before he even wanted to.

"So, what now?" Kara asked.

Cheryl threw her hands into the air. "I have no idea. I

don't even know how to bring any of this up. I don't even know if he wants me to anymore."

"Well . . . has he given any hints that he regrets any of your arguments?"

"He called me after he landed last night."

"And?"

"Basically demanded I tell him what was holding me back from him."

Kara jumped up. "There! That was it. Why would he do that if he didn't want to be a part of your life anymore? The guy is falling in love with you, Cheryl. He wants to see how things go for the two of you. Even after all the rejections he's had, he's putting himself out there. He just can't put himself out too far without some encouragement from you."

Cheryl nodded. She'd already come to believe that. "What do I do, then?"

"Go find him. Tell him your feelings and thoughts. Give him the biggest kiss he's ever had."

"I don't know where he lives."

"But you do know where he works. Start there."

Good idea. "I should do that now, right?"

"Of course. Good luck! Let me know how it goes."

Cheryl gave Kara a quick hug, then got into her car and drove to her mom's facility. She parked in the first spot she found, hopped out of her car, and ran through the front doors to the check-in desk.

"Is Dr. Lincoln here?" Ugh! Now *she* was calling him that too.

"Check his office—he could be there. Or he might be meeting with patients. Today was his first day back after vacation, so he's been hammered."

"Thank you."

Cheryl hurried in the direction the receptionist had pointed and found Lincoln's office. It was empty. Instead of sitting and waiting, she walked up and down every hall of the facility, glancing in the open doors as she went.

Lincoln wasn't anywhere.

Cheryl finally made her way to her mom's room, disappointment crashing over her. Now that she'd finally decided to act, she wanted to do something about it. She didn't want to risk losing her nerve or changing her mind.

She didn't *think* she'd change her mind, but she had a crazy way of talking herself out of plans if she dwelt on them too much. No way was she allowing that to happen. She'd stalk him to his house if necessary. She was sure she could torture his address out of one of his employees. Or beg it from them. Surely someone would take pity on her.

Helen was eating dinner when Cheryl got there. "Mom!" she said, stepping to her mother's side and giving her a half-hug, careful not to knock over any food.

"I'm so happy to see you! You just missed Lincoln."

"That's *Dr.* Lincoln to you," Cheryl said, grinning at her mom. "Did he say where he was going?"

"Nope."

"Did he say when he'd be back?"

"Nope."

Cheryl doubted that. "Seriously?"

"I'm a patient. He doesn't tell me anything, dear."

"I don't buy that for one minute." Cheryl studied her mom's face, noticing the grin for the first time. "Oh, boy. You've been conniving again, haven't you?"

"Who, me? Never. I wouldn't stoop that low."

Cheryl put her hand on her mom's arm and leaned closer to her. "You'd better tell me what you know. What's going on?"

"I can't say anything."

"Why not?"

"Because I promised. I don't back out on promises."

"Fine. Be that way." Cheryl folded her arms and mock pouted. "But if this destroys my relationship with Lincoln, I'm blaming you for the rest of my life."

"*If* it destroys your relationship, it wasn't that much of a relationship."

Cheryl waited for a moment, but Helen resumed eating, pointedly ignoring her daughter, so she decided to head back to the front desk again. The receptionist looked up just as she was hanging up the phone. "That was Dr. Lincoln. He's on a date right now and won't be back to work until tomorrow."

Cheryl blinked. He was on a *date*? How was that possible? He'd just gotten back from Hawaii, for crying out loud, where he'd been kissing her. If he had a girlfriend waiting at home, she'd . . . she'd punch him. "Did he say who it was with?"

The receptionist gave her an expression that showed she clearly thought it was none of Cheryl's business. "No, but there were laughing teenagers in the background."

Cheryl frowned. *Teenagers* in the background? What the heck? He was on a date with a woman who had kids? Or maybe it was one of his sisters.

That thought spiked hope in Cheryl's mind.

Her phone dinged with an incoming text, and she pulled it out to see it was Xander.

Where are you mom?

Visiting Grandma.

Good. We just pulled up. Want to hang out with us?

Cheryl tried to tamp down the disappointment that crashed over her. Her conversation with Lincoln could wait until tomorrow. She hadn't seen her kids in days, and she missed them.

Sure. Let's go see a movie.

Cheryl turned and left the building, looking for Jack's car. Presumably the kids would be with him, since they'd all been camping that week.

A black stretch limo blocked her view of the parking lot, though. As she started around it, the back door opened, and Xander jumped out, followed by Jade. They rushed to her side.

"He's so awesome, Mom!" Xander said. "You *have* to date him."

"And *marry* him!" Jade said, gripping her mom's arm.

Lincoln stepped out of the limo, blushing. "I didn't tell them to say any of that, I promise."

Cheryl felt as if her heart had stopped. "You've been hanging out with my kids?" A weird pressure started at her chest, causing all sorts of emotions to spread through her body. Shock, excitement, wonder, and love. Definitely love.

Lincoln nodded, his blush deepening. "Pretty much all day."

"But your receptionist said . . ."

"That I'd been scrambling at work? That I was on a date? Yup. I know."

"You told her to tell me that?"

He grinned. "Sure did."

"Why?"

He stepped to her, close enough to touch, but not making contact. "Because I wanted to surprise you."

"You did?"

Lincoln nodded. "Cheryl . . ." He paused for several seconds, then took a deep breath.

"Man up, dude," Xander said.

Lincoln mock rolled his eyes, then motioned to the teen, glancing at Cheryl. "*This* is what you put up with?"

Cheryl saw the grin under his pretend irritation. "All day, every day."

"Man. Tough life."

"You have no idea."

They studied each other for several moments, both smiling. Cheryl's heart swelled to nearly bursting at the acceptance she saw there. At the fact that he'd been spending time with her kids. That they approved of him. That *he* approved of *them*.

"Can we go for a walk?" he asked.

Cheryl turned to her kids and gave them both quick hugs. "I love you, I missed you. Wait in the limo for us?"

The teens nodded and hopped back inside, and Cheryl turned her attention to Lincoln. He took her by the hand and led her through the parking lot and to the street. Neither of them said anything for several moments, giving Cheryl a chance to recognize just how good it felt to be holding his hand again. It was so right, so perfect.

"Cheryl," Lincoln started, "please tell me all of your concerns about us. Be one hundred percent open and honest and don't worry about my feelings. I need to understand how you function so I can better align myself."

"So you can tell me what you think I want to hear?" She said it as gently as she could, but she needed him to be aware of how well she knew his personality.

He shook his head. "I do that with people in general . . . but only when the outcome doesn't matter. With serious situations, I will always find a way to be honest. Even if it means thinking things over for a few hours or even a day or two before answering, or fumbling through my answer to figure out where I stand. You will always, always know my genuine thoughts. I like to maintain harmony, but not at the expense of honesty."

Cheryl studied Lincoln's face for a few moments, wondering how accurate what he'd said was. She saw nothing but open truth there.

"I'm worried we're not good for each other."

He nodded. "A fair concern—one I've had myself."

"But that's not something I can figure out after only a couple days of dating." It seemed pretty obvious. "So I don't give it a lot of weight now. But I'm also worried I've built you up too much over the years."

"That's also a really good concern. But it's also something you'll figure out as we date each other." He glanced at her. "I hope what you find out about me ends up being as good as you'd imagined."

She gave him a half smile. "So far, you're better in some ways. You've matured a lot since high school."

He laughed. "I should hope so. It would be sad if I were still the same boy from back then."

"In a few ways, you are."

He hesitated. "What do you mean?"

"You're excited, enthusiastic, and you still love pretty much everyone. Because of that, people are drawn to you."

"But?"

"You're not flippant and immature, anymore. You weren't ever badly flippant, but you did have a streak of . . . well, kind of cruelty, when it came to the jokes you played at our teachers' expense. You have so much more depth now than you had back then. You empathize with others' difficult experiences."

"Hard times will do that to a person." He kept his gaze forward. "I hope what I've gone through hasn't changed me in a negative way. I've worried about that a lot. We can discuss my feelings on that topic more in a bit, when we've talked through your feelings, but it's been a struggle for me."

"Your experiences haven't negatively changed you—at least, you didn't allow them to, from what I can tell. They've made you more vulnerable, more sensitive. Both of those traits are good for a man to have." At least to a point. She didn't want someone more sensitive than she was—that wouldn't be a good combination. She grinned to herself.

"Good to know." He was silent for a moment, obviously thinking over her words. "Anything else?"

She sighed. "I *am* worried about you working with other women. I know it's petty and immature of me, but—"

Lincoln stopped walking and turned to face her, putting his hands on her shoulders. "Cheryl, wanting reassurance in a relationship is not wrong. It's not petty, and it's not immature. How I handled that whole situation was harsh and inappropriate. I'm embarrassed by the things I said. I was seeking validation myself, and I didn't give it to you when you needed it." He shook his head, obviously mad at himself. "I'm ashamed of how I behaved."

He took both of her hands, and oh, how right, how good it felt.

Lincoln continued talking. "I'm incredibly loyal—to a fault, where even quitting a miserable job is concerned. It's hard on me. I have never cheated—never even been tempted to. When I choose to love a woman, she is literally the only thing I see. I *notice* attractive women, but they hold zero power over me." He leaned in, not breaking eye contact, his expression serious. "When I give someone my heart, it is theirs forever."

Cheryl's eyes filled with tears, and she dropped her gaze, not comfortable crying in front of him. He seemed to realize she needed some time because he wrapped his arms around her and held her while she sorted her emotions.

Everything he'd said so far had been honest, and it touched the parts of her heart where she was the most insecure. She felt the final walls dropping as he rubbed her back, the warmth from his chest and arms enveloping her.

He cleared his throat. "Anything else?"

"Not on my part," she said, feeling it to her core. "You've already shown me you don't mind kids, and that was one of my biggest things. So let's discuss your concerns now."

She felt his Adam's apple bob as he swallowed. "They seem so petty."

Cheryl leaned back and placed a hand on his cheek, looking up into his eyes. "They're not. I promise."

He took a deep breath. "Okay. All right. Where to begin."

"Oh, no. That many?"

He shook his head. "It's all based on the experiences I've had where women are concerned."

She studied him, waiting for him to continue. Instead, he turned and started walking, and she followed.

"Originally," he said, "I was worried I'd have to constantly reassure you of my love for you. That there would be no end to your hesitations—that you'd never get to the point where you trusted me."

Cheryl's brain had to scramble to get caught up with the rest of what he'd said after he'd mentioned the word "love." He *loved* her? Holy smokes! Wow. He'd said the word earlier, but it hadn't been about *her*. Not per se, anyway.

Lincoln was still talking. "But I've come to recognize that reassurance really *is* an important part of a relationship. And just because I feel comfortable doesn't mean you will too." He looked at her. "I can't make you choose to trust me, but I *can* be more patient. To not want to jump the gun while also saying we need to take things a day at a time." He growled. "So much conflict in me— wanting things to happen right now, but freaking out at the idea that they might."

"It's pretty normal," she said. She'd definitely been there herself.

She felt her heart swell again at the validation he was giving her for her feelings in Hawaii.

Lincoln continued. "We'll need to be patient with each other as we feel things out. And . . ." He hesitated. "There's something else I haven't told you about myself."

Cheryl's heart practically stopped. What could it be? She had no idea—she couldn't even make a guess.

"What's that?" she asked, keeping her tone light.

"My concerns about marriage."

Her eyes widened. "Marriage?"

"Not between a man and a woman, but marriage for me. After all the rejections I had, I started assuming a greater power didn't want me to get hitched. That it wasn't in the cards for me. I mean, some people never find a spouse. Why would I be so arrogant as to always assume I would?"

Cheryl rubbed the back of his hand with her thumb. "It's not arrogance—it's human nature to want to be with someone."

"It really is. I've come to understand that without marriage, I'm stuck. I can't grow. And I find it almost impossible to believe that God would want me to stop progressing."

He turned to her. "I don't know what's in the stars for me, but the past few days have given me a reason to hope that I was wrong. That being truly happy is possible for me. That finding someone who would complete me could happen."

Cheryl's eyes started swimming with tears again. She knew he was referring to her.

"Hawaii was the happiest I've been in years," he said. "And I'm scared spitless I ruined things permanently by wallowing in my insecurities."

Cheryl smiled at his use of the word "spitless," but she sobered up pretty quickly as she saw the turmoil on his face. "You haven't messed things up—not even close. I made some pretty dumb mistakes too, and I've realized that. I've realized that not all of my insecurities are as big as I think they are."

Cheryl put her arms around his neck. "Lincoln, I'm sorry for everything you've been through. I'm sorry that your relationships led you to wonder if God wanted you to be miserable. And I'm so sorry I pushed you to have those thoughts only days into our relationship. Would you forgive me?"

Lincoln stepped closer, tucking a finger under her chin, raising her face.

"There's nothing to forgive. I love you, Cheryl. And I promise I'll love you forever. That I'll love your kids too. That I'll never leave your side, unless you ask me to. That I'll bring you breakfast in bed and cook dinners for you as much as you want and need it. That I'll support you through the pains of raising teenagers. That I won't do anything to get between you and your kids."

Her shoulders shook as tears spilled over her cheeks. This man truly understood her. "I . . . I love you too. I've always loved you, even when I hated you." She wasn't sure what else to say—she'd never been good at words like he was. "That won't ever change. As long as you want me, I'll want you, and even if you stop wanting me."

He shook his head. "I won't. I've never been surer about something than I am about us. I know it's early in our relationship, but I can see us working toward marriage."

Cheryl's heart swelled even more—so much where she felt like her ribs would break from the pressure. "You can?" she whispered. She'd known that was what this conversation was about, but actually hearing him say it felt like icing on the cake.

He nodded. "I can." He put his arms around her, pulling her close and looking into her eyes. "Like I said earlier, I want to spend the rest of my life with you."

"That would be pretty awesome."

It was all she *could* say. She prayed he'd see the love in her eyes, though. And when he gave her a quiet smile, tucking a loose strand of hair behind her ear, she knew he understood.

Lincoln kissed her softly, gently. She wrapped her arms around his neck and pulled him close. She couldn't get enough of him—of this man who'd stood her up years earlier, who'd taught her more about herself than any other person, who'd fallen in love with her despite her flaws, her boring life, her hectic situation.

Who loved her *because* of those things.

She couldn't wait to begin forever with him.

EPILOGUE

TWO WEEKS LATER

*L*incoln dropped to a sitting position on the couch, pulling Cheryl down with him, nestling her against his side, wrapping an arm around her.

"Everyone ready?" Xander asked.

"Yup!" Jade said, bowl of popcorn in her hands.

Xander sighed with exaggeration. "*Finally.*"

Cheryl and Lincoln chuckled. The teen had been trying to arrange a movie night with everyone for days. Schedules had finally clicked into place, the movie was ready, and no one had anywhere else to go.

Xander flipped off the lights and started the show. "Jade, if you get scared, let me know, and I'll turn off the movie."

Jade scoffed. "Dude, I'm almost fifteen. Nothing scares me anymore."

Lincoln raised an eyebrow. "Nothing?" he asked.

"Nothing."

Cheryl looked up at Lincoln, a stern expression on her face. "Don't even think about it," she said, obviously knowing where his thoughts had gone.

Man, she knew him too well. "Awww, can't I do just one little prank?"

"Not even one."

"You're so boring."

"I'm the worst."

Lincoln laughed. He'd really hit it off with Xander and Jade, and he knew it meant the world to Cheryl. It had been easy to love them, though—they fit seamlessly into the future he envisioned with her.

He tilted her face up and placed a kiss on her lips, loving how soft and inviting they were. He tried not to get carried away, but apparently, Xander and Jade had lower thresholds than he expected because after only a few seconds, groans surrounded them.

"Get a room, guys," Xander said. He froze, staring at his mom. "I mean, uh . . . don't get a room. Go sit in the car if you want to kiss."

Jade had a horrified expression on her face as she stared at her brother. "'Get a *room*?' That's *disgusting*, Xander."

He put his hands up. "Sorry, it's just a saying."

Lincoln and Cheryl both laughed before Lincoln turned back to Cheryl. "Maybe we *should* get a room."

Her eyes widened. "No milk for you unless you pay for the cow."

He laughed. "I totally and completely intend on doing exactly that."

"Did you just call me a cow?" Cheryl said with a mock glare.

He put his hands up. "Hey! Those were your words."

She grinned at him. "If you can prank, so can I."

"Fair enough."

Lincoln pulled her against him, satisfaction flooding

his system. He couldn't believe how wonderful his life was now. Cheryl had calmed his fears, loved him through his anxiety, and had been by him every step of the way. She'd been patient with his work hours and had helped him find another physical therapist to help with the load.

She'd proven her love over and over again. He couldn't wait to ask her to be his wife, and he planned to do it soon.

His younger self would have scoffed at how quickly it had happened. But present Lincoln had learned something. Sometimes, leaping before you see every step of the way ensures you the future you want, whereas hesitation could mean losing what you want the most.

And he wasn't about to lose Cheryl again.

THE END

Would you like to read Lincoln's proposal to Cheryl? Get it for free in a box set from my website (www.andreapearsonbooks.com) when you join my readers group. The box set has a bunch of other awesome epilogues featuring characters in the Alpine Hospital Romance books. Plus, it has Dean Harrison's complete story, which is guaranteed to make you giggle and swoon. :-)

As an FYI, Lincoln's proposal is based on how my brother proposed to his wife. My brother is a big tease too, and Cheryl's response is pretty similar to my sister-in-law's. I think you'll get a kick out of it. :-)

AUTHOR NOTE

Hi, everyone! I hope you enjoyed *Romancing Dr. Lincoln*. Cheryl's plight strikes a chord for me. We're the same age, and yet, my oldest (as of this writing) is only 9, whereas Cheryl's kids are teenagers. I frequently wonder what happened to the life I always dreamed of—which was very similar to Cheryl's dreams. Growing up, I wanted nothing more than to get married in my early twenties and have a bunch of kids and a husband with a standard nine-to-five. I definitely don't regret the turn my life took, but I do wish I hadn't been alone for so many years. (I was only 29 when Nolan and I got married, but dang, those years in my twenties were hard! He was 32.)

A happy thing about this book, though—my husband and I went to Hawaii for our ten-year anniversary, and we stayed in the house where Lincoln and Cheryl stayed. We visited the beaches they walked and went to the volcano and the black-sand beach and kissed and had such a wonderful time that I knew I'd need to have characters take that same trip in a book someday. Delving into the

Big Island again, but through my characters' eyes was so much fun.

Anyway, life doesn't always go how we want it to, but there's still so much joy to be found in it. I'm so glad Cheryl and Lincoln have found their happiness. I hope you have too.

Thanks to my physical therapist for answering my questions and helping me figure out how to make Lincoln believable as a physical therapist. (And also, thanks to myself for constantly getting injured or having surgeries that land me in physical therapy every year so I had the chance to ask my questions. :-D)

I plan to write many more books about Alpine Hospital. I hope you'll come along for the journey! Join my readers group (www.andreapearsonbooks.com) for some free stories and for info on when my next book will come out. :-)

Much love!

Andrea Kate

ABOUT THE AUTHOR

Andrea Kate Pearson, author of the Alpine Hospital Romance series under this name and *USA Today* bestselling author of urban fantasy under the name Andrea Pearson, lives with her husband and children in a small valley framed with hills. She is an avid reader and outdoor enthusiast who plays several instruments, not including the banjo, and loves putting together musical arrangements. Her favorite sports are basketball and football, though several knee surgeries and incurably awful coordination prevent her from playing them.

Andrea spends as much time with her husband and kids as possible. Favorite activities include painting, watching movies, collecting and listening to music, and discussing books and authors.

Check out her available sweet romances on Amazon.